THE START OF US

T.K. CHAPIN

Branch Publishing

To claim a FREE Christian Romance visit offer.tkchapin.com

Version: 05.9.2019

ISBN: 1097562077

ISBN-13: 978-1097562077

Dedicated to my loving wife.
For all the years she has put up with me
And many more to come.

CONTENTS

In their hearts humans plan their course,
but the Lord establishes their steps.
Proverbs 16:9

CHAPTER 1

*N*atalie Townsend had known what it was to love and what it was to hate, but she hadn't known what it was to *be* fully loved. She hadn't left her bed in the two hours she had already been awake. It was her day off from the Verizon call center in Spokane, but she didn't have any reason to get up. Her soul had grown so weary of the repetitiveness that life had handed her. She didn't know how much longer she could endure. Did she deserve a life that felt more like a prison sentence? Sometimes, she felt like she did. Maybe if she was kinder to her ex-husband, God would have been a little bit more gracious toward her after the divorce. Maybe if she had volunteered down at the soup kitchen on Friday nights, her life could've been different. Regardless of what she could've done, should've done, or would've done, this was Natalie's lot in life now and she knew it. She could feel it in her bones with each new day.

Smokey, her charcoal-colored two-year-old cat, suddenly leaped onto her bed and purred as he maneuvered across the quilt her mother had made for her when she was a child. Natalie's feline friend found his resting place by her neck.

Nuzzling in, he got comfortable in the spot right between her shoulder and cheek bone.

The warmth of a living creature was a welcomed presence to her. A faint smile broke on Natalie's soft pink lips as she lifted a hand to pet Smokey. Tilting her head, a few strands of her disheveled brown hair fell across her emerald-green eyes and cheek. She reached up and pushed the strands behind her ear and looked lovingly at her cat. Smokey was the closest thing to a friend Natalie had these days. Most of her days were filled with work, and her evenings usually consisted of binge-watching a series on Netflix while eating her way through a pint of her favorite Ben & Jerry's ice cream. Natalie often found herself wondering if this was all life would be from now on. A part of her clung to the possibility that God had something more for her in store.

Finally rising from her bed that morning, Natalie went into the en-suite bathroom and drew a hot bath. Tossing in two lavender bath salts, she let herself inhale the sweet aroma rising from the flowing steamy water. The scent conjured a bittersweet memory of her grandmother's lavender bush on the side of the farmhouse out in Chattaroy, a small community just a short drive from Spokane. As a girl, she had frequented her grandparents' farm with her parents on almost a weekly basis. That all changed when she grew up, but even more so since her grandmother had passed away five years ago. She hadn't been out there more than a few times, the most recent visit a month ago. She wasn't particularly close to her grandfather, Clay, like she had been with her grandmother.

Climbing into her bath water, she slid beneath the surface to where only her head stuck out a small fraction. Turning the knob of the tub's faucet with her toes, the squeak of the metal sounded and brought the deafening silence back to her life, back to the present moment.

Natalie thought of work. Her job was uninteresting, and most days, she disliked even being there, but when she was home, she didn't like that either. No matter where she was, she couldn't find the least bit of joy. Her existence on the planet Earth lacked purpose and meaning. Contentment and joy were out of reach. She prayed for these things to somehow come to her, but God hadn't answered those requests. She figured He was probably busy with someone far more important than little ol' Natalie Townsend.

Hearing her phone suddenly ring in her bedroom just outside the doorway of the bathroom caused her to flinch. Startled by the sound, she pushed her head further out of the water but remained in the tub. Craning her neck for a moment toward the doorway, she thought, *Probably just another bill collector*. Rising further out of the water, she reached over the side of the bathtub and retrieved a romance novel she had been reading for the last couple of weeks. Opening the pages, she began to let her mind escape her life and bleak existence. She let herself take the form of another, someone much happier than her, someone with a far more interesting story than hers.

After her bath, Natalie got dressed and picked up her cell phone from the nightstand in her bedroom.

She raised an eyebrow. It was a missed call from her father, Gerald. Tapping the message to listen, she put the phone up to her ear.

"Hey. I know I said we'd get together for dinner one of these nights, but I've been swamped at the office with some big clients lately. Anyway, I . . . need to talk to you about something. Come on over to the house if you get this message before five today." He paused for a moment. "It's Saturday, June 29th."

Her father was extremely preoccupied by his work and his second wife, Chrissy. When he wasn't busy at work, it seemed like Gerald and Chrissy were always off on some cruise or visiting this city or that city. He had a life, and Natalie was jealous, not only of his ability to move on past his marriage with her mom, but of how easily and quickly he was able to heal and find new love. Natalie's heart hadn't fully healed from losing her mother or her first husband, Martin.

For the first year following her divorce from Martin, Natalie spent every night crying herself to sleep over what had happened. The second year, she got mad and proceeded to throw out every reminder of him in her life. Now, though, at year three, she was like a traveler roaming through a life of what had been and never would be. Natalie didn't know where she belonged anymore. Her mom was dead, her father busy, and her sibling, Gwen, was on the other side of the country with her husband and kids. She was utterly and hopelessly alone.

Hanging up from the voicemail, Natalie slipped her feet into a pair of flip-flops and grabbed her purse from the counter in the kitchen. Going to see her dad was a welcomed light in the otherwise dark cycle of life she had been stuck in.

Arriving at the towering oak doors of her father's home twenty minutes later, Natalie knocked and waited outside. Her father, Gerald, was a wealthy real estate investor and was moving more properties in the greater Spokane area than anyone else at the time.

Chrissy answered the door.

"Natalie!" Throwing open her arms, Chrissy stepped across the threshold and wrapped herself around Natalie, giving her a squeeze slightly beyond comfortable.

"Hey, Chrissy. My dad home?"

Releasing her, Chrissy nodded and brought her inside into the foyer. "Yes, he's up in his study. We haven't seen you in a while! How is the job at . . ."

"The call center—it's going fine." Smiling politely, Natalie walked with Chrissy through the foyer toward the wraparound stairs that led up to the study. "I'll just go up."

"Okay. Nice seeing you again!"

Natalie's smile fell away as she climbed the wooden staircase. Chrissy was a nice woman, and Natalie had even grown to like her somewhat, but she'd never replace her mother. Her heart was glad that Chrissy loved her father dearly, and that fact alone was enough for Natalie to be okay with her.

Reaching the top of the staircase, she continued down the hallway to her father's study. Knocking lightly, she entered.

Her dad smiled up at her as he continued a conversation on his desk phone. He held out a finger, indicating to Natalie that he'd be ready to chat in a moment.

Walking over to the bookcase in her father's study, Natalie browsed his collection to see if anything new had been added.

The phone clicked as her father set it down on the receiver.

"Hey, Pumpkin. I'm glad you made it."

Her eyes lit and her heart warmed at hearing the old childhood nickname given to her by her father. Knowing now that he wanted something, she broke into a grin as she walked over to his desk.

"What do you want, Dad?"

Letting out a laugh, he stood up and raised his eyebrows. "How'd you know I want something?"

"You haven't called me that since I was sixteen. So, what . . . twelve years ago?" Natalie laughed.

Nodding, he came around the desk and sat partially on the front of it as he crossed his arms. "This is true. I do have a favor to ask of you, sweetheart."

Her heart flickered with a small flame of hope. "You need *me* to do something?"

"I do."

Her inner spirit radiated with the joyful prospect of being useful. "All right. I'll bite. What is it?"

"Your grandfather Clay's health is in decline."

Her heart weakened. "Oh, Dad . . . I went out there last month and I tried to help, but there's only so much I can do in a single Saturday afternoon. I told you he needs help long-term."

"I know." He nodded and a frown set into his face. "I investigated what you told me. I even took a trip out there myself. You were right, Pumpkin. He does need ongoing help. And full-time help at that!"

Seeing where the conversation was heading, she shook her head. "I have a job. I can't do that."

"Right. That's why I asked you over. I know you want to go back to school. You've regretted dropping out since your divorce, and I can help you with that. All I'm asking in return is that you help me with your grandfather."

"You know how I feel about getting handouts, Dad."

Standing up from the edge of the desk, her father took a step closer to her. "I know you don't want anything for free, and that's not what this is. It's an opportunity for *both* of us."

"But why wouldn't you just hire a nurse or housekeeper? That would be a lot cheaper than paying for school."

"That wouldn't be family. I think he needs family right now. You are perfect for it, in my mind."

Peering into her father's eyes, she let the idea process through her mind for a moment. She'd be able to go back to school and get her degree that she had given up on when she decided to marry Martin. That free ride for great grades had been lost down the drain of bad decisions. This was another chance at school, another chance at getting a real career, and most of all, another chance at life.

Raising her eyebrows as her interest grew, she looked at her father directly. "How would it work?"

"It would be simple. You would move out to the farm and live with your grandfather."

"I don't want to do online school, Dad. I need a classroom environment."

He held his hands up. "That's fine. I'm confident that even going to school, you will have enough time to spend with him when you're not in classes. All I ask is that you live with your grandfather and take care of him when you can. He just needs help with laundry and food. Feeding the cows. You know."

"Oh, Grandpa and his cows . . ."

Her dad smiled and let out a light laugh. "Yeah. Your grandfather is strong-willed, and a lot like you. He won't give up." Going back around his desk to his swivel chair, he picked up his phone. Before putting it to his ear, he looked up at her. "So, you'll do it?"

"Yeah. I will."

Smiling at her father, Natalie was washed with love as he reflected the smile back at her and started to dial on the phone as he spoke. "I'll have a truck arranged to move your things out there this weekend."

"Wait." Taking a step closer to the desk, she pressed her hand against the top of the desk as her pulse raced.

"Yeah?"

"What about my apartment? What if things don't work out or . . . ?" She didn't want to say it, but the look in his eyes told her that he knew her thoughts about Grandpa passing. "I'd just feel more comfortable with a fallback plan."

He agreed and placed the phone back onto the receiver. "That's true. Tell you what. You take what you need out there, and I'll pay to keep your apartment in good standing with rent."

Natalie smiled. "Thank you, Dad."

After exchanging goodbyes with her father, she left his study and traveled back down the staircase to the foyer and through the front door. As Natalie walked out to her car in the driveway, she imagined what school would be like. Her thoughts drifted to one day becoming a graphic designer and living in a nice flat in a big city somewhere. Her heart's flame of hope grew. Things were looking up, and she turned her gaze to the clouds outside her dad's house. *Thank you, God.*

BUTTONING HIS JEANS FRANTICALLY, Jacob Stilts grabbed a white folded V-neck from the top shelf of his closet and quickly put it on. Jaw clenched as he thought about it being Saturday, his one and only day to sleep in when the markets weren't open in New York, he stormed out from his bedroom. Cutting through the living room, he bolted for the front door. Flinging the door open, he glared at the 2,400-pound intruder on his property—a cow named Betsy. He could tell it was her because her left eye had a dark patch of hair on it.

Walking down the cement path leading from his cabin, Jacob began to yell. "You need to stop coming over here and eating up my garden, Betsy!"

The cow lifted her head and looked over at him as it continued to chew on a tomato, seeming to have no care in the world.

Jacob's cabin out in the country was supposed to be a place of solitude and peace, a place in which he could reconnect with God and rediscover what it meant to be chosen by the Almighty. It may have only been three-quarters of an acre out in the country, but to Jacob, it was three-quarters of an acre in paradise. Betsy, though, along with a few of her cow friends, posed a real threat to this life of tranquil living.

"Skit! C'mon. Go!"

Working the cow out from his garden, he walked with it through the field, guiding it back home toward the farm. As he walked the field on his way over to the neighbor's farm, he formulated his words for the owner, Clay Townsend. He had been more than patient with the old man since he had gotten a good deal on buying a small portion of land from him over a year ago, but Jacob's patience was running thin the last couple of months. Betsy and company had been in his yard on several occasions now, and Clay still hadn't fixed the fence to prevent the problem from reoccurring.

Once to the farm across the field, Jacob placed Betsy in the barn and then headed to the farmhouse to have a talk with Clay. Finding the old man outside, struggling in his attempts to refill a bird feeder on the porch, Jacob approached.

"Hi, Jake."

"Hello." Helping Clay, Jacob took the bird feeder and latched it onto the hook hanging near the roof's edge. Then, he turned toward his neighbor. "Listen, Betsy got into my yard again. She was just munching away in my garden."

Clay laughed, nodding as he raised his bushy eyebrows. "I told you she loves tomatoes."

"This isn't funny, Clay. It's serious."

Straightening up, Clay nodded but seemed tired. "Sorry."

"Look, I don't want to be mean, but it's getting more and more frequent. Can't you fix the fence so it stops?"

Uneasiness rested in the old man's eyes. Then he peered past Jacob toward the barn, then back at him. "I guess there's no point in hiding it from you any longer. I'm sick."

His insides flinched. "What?"

"I'm not trying to get out of the responsibility for my

cows, but I think you should know I'm not up to par like I once was, and the reason is because I'm dying." The old man let out a ragged sigh. "Have been for a while, but the cancer is getting more aggressive. I'm losing strength. I promise I am truly sorry about the fence and the cows."

"I am so sorry, Clay. I had no idea. You know what? I can fix that fence! I'll get my tools, watch a video, and get it done for you."

"No, please don't. I don't need your pity, just your understanding." Finding a seat on a worn-out wicker chair on the porch, Clay shook his head. "You don't need to worry about the fence, boy. My granddaughter from Spokane is coming to take care of things around here for me. She'll get it done."

Light laughter filled Jacob's voice. "A city gal?"

Clay's eyes connected with Jacob's. "She's tougher than most girls, Jake. She'll get it taken care of, I'm sure of it."

Cancer was still stuck in Jacob's thought processes and he sat down beside the old man. Turning toward him, he raised his eyebrows. "Is your cancer treatable? Or are you on a time limit or something? Hope you don't mind me asking."

"It's okay to ask. The doctors are saying nine months or less. Maybe longer, maybe shorter."

"You seem rather calm about it all."

A genuine smile broke on Clay's face, and he peered out at the hundred-plus-year-old oak tree sitting a few feet from the porch. "I've lived a good life and a blessed one by God. I'm at peace with going home."

"Wow. I love the Lord too, but I couldn't imagine being *ready* to go."

Folding his arms, Clay kept his smile as he nodded lightly. "Once your heart has been bonded together with a woman through marriage and you have lived a full life together, you'll experience the deepest kind of love that exists. Through my marriage, I didn't just learn how much I can love my wife. I learned how much God loves us. I can only define this kind of love as divine and supernatural. Then one day, you lose that love. When that happens, a part of you dies. Then, and only then, you'll understand being ready to go. You see, Jake. My truest and everlasting love, my Lord and Savior Jesus Christ, is now the love I look forward to, and I am ready to meet Him face to face."

Jacob rose to his feet and peered at Clay as he held a joyful expression on his face. "I hope one day, I'll experience the kind of love you speak of, Clay."

"Oh, I'm sure you will, Jake. Someday, you'll have your very own Rose."

Hearing a car pull into the driveway, Jacob turned his head to see a woman driving over the bridge that stretched over the creek. The woman parked in front of the shrubs and trees that outlined the old man's yard.

"I'd better head home. Take care of yourself."

Clay stood up and shook his hand. "Meet my grand-daughter."

He shook his head. "That's okay. I have to get going."

"All right. Thanks for bringing Betsy back."

Tipping Clay a nod, he said, "You're welcome." Then he left the porch.

On his way back toward the white wood fence that separated the field from the yard, Jacob glanced over his shoulder to see a woman with wavy brown hair walking up the path leading toward the farmhouse, holding a cat. *She's cute,* he thought for a moment before brushing the thought away.

CHAPTER 2

*a*fter settling into the guest bedroom upstairs in the farmhouse, Natalie came downstairs and started making breakfast for her grandfather while he sat at the kitchen table. She hadn't been able to dislodge the image of the attractive mystery man jumping the fence when she first arrived at her grandfather's house earlier that morning.

Looking over her shoulder toward Clay from the stove, Natalie raised an eyebrow. "Who was that jumping your fence and going into the field this morning?"

"My neighbor, Jake. He bought a piece of my land a little over a year ago."

"I see. I don't recall your mentioning him before." She turned back to the skillet of eggs.

"Didn't seem relevant."

As she finished cooking the eggs and slid them onto a plate for her grandpa, she kept thinking about the man. She walked over to the table and set the plate of eggs down in front of Clay. "What's his story, anyway?"

Clay's eyes lifted toward her with a smile. "Are you interested in the boy?"

Laughing, she shook her head as she smiled. "No, not at all. It'd just be good to know who's living next door. I'll be living here too, and a girl can never be too safe these days."

"Fair enough. Well, I can't tell you much about him, as I haven't a lot of information. I know he's thirty and moved here from New York City. Oh, and he works from home. He's a good Christian man too. Attends church up the road at the little community church I go to. Oh, one other thing. He doesn't seem to like cows."

Lightly laughing, Natalie sat down at the table. "Cows?"

Clay grinned. "Betsy keeps getting out and eating up his garden. It seems to bother him a lot. Which reminds me. I'll need you to find the hole in the barbed-wire fence where she's getting out and fix it."

"Okay. I can do that."

After starting in on laundry a little while later, Natalie then watched a YouTube video on how to repair a barbed-wire fence. Feeling like an expert of fence repair, she proceeded out to the garage near the barn to gather the tools needed for the repair. Loading what she needed into the back of the farm truck, she got in and drove over to the gate. Parking, she got out and opened the gate that led into the field. Peering across the fields and even the hill, her lips curled into a smile. It brought her heart a measure of joy to be back in the fresh country air instead of sitting in a cubicle at the Verizon call center in Spokane.

The chains in which she had felt trapped were loosening and falling off all around her. The depression that plagued her heart and mind was lifting, and there was a bright hope shining for her now. School was still a couple of months off, but just being at the farm for that first few hours was stirring within her a new focus and hope.

Getting back into the truck, she shut the door and continued to drive through the opening and into the field. As she followed the fence line further into the field, she spotted Jacob walking to her far right side. He was heading toward a section of the fence. Squinting, she leaned to get a better look.

She noticed him carrying a tool box.

Cranking the wheel, Natalie turned and cut through the field to make her way over to him. Not following the grooved path carved out by years of her grandfather traveling the same route made for a bumpy ride. Natalie bobbed up and down as she made her way toward Jacob. Finally arriving at his location, she noticed he had gone right to the spot in the fence where the cows were getting through. Parking, she got out.

"Hey! I have this taken care of. You can go home."

Raising an eyebrow, he shook his head. "That's all right. I'm already here and fixing it."

Frustrated, she approached him. "Dude, it's fine. I will take care of it."

Stopping, he turned toward her. He looked into her eyes and for a moment, she didn't feel lonely anymore. His big golden-brown eyes were a place of warmth and comfort.

"You're a stubborn woman, aren't you?"

Displeased with his comment, she scoffed and broke eye contact. "No, I am here to take care of my grandpa and his farm. You're in the way."

"I've lived out here for a while now and I've never seen you. If you don't mind, I'd rather handle this myself and make sure it gets done right."

Her anger flared, furthering the dampening of her good mood. She put a hand on her hip. "What is *that* supposed to mean? *Get it done right?* Is that some kind of jab at me because I'm a woman?" Tapping her chin, she gave him a short nod and leaned in. "Maybe you're right, Jake. Maybe they only teach people how to fix fences back in New York City."

He let out a laugh and smiled as he turned toward her fully. Hands up in the air, he looked into her eyes again. "Okay. You got me. I YouTube'd a video before I came out."

Smiling as her frustration melted away, she nodded and pulled her cell phone out from her pocket with the queued video on the screen. "So did I."

They both laughed.

"How about we work on it together?" He dipped his eyes and smiled. "I didn't quite catch your name."

"Natalie, and all right. I can do that."

They started to work on the fence together. Glancing back toward the direction of the farm, Jacob raised an eyebrow about five minutes in. He looked at her again, causing her heart to pound. "So, you're here to help your grandpa out for a while?"

She looked over at him. "Yeah."

"Just curious, but what made you agree to do it? I can't imagine most people would be willing, let alone have the time, to put their life on hold to do a thing like that."

"He's my grandpa, and in exchange for my doing this, my father is helping me go back to school." She hesitated to share the fact that her life was more boring than watching water dry on hot cement. "And a break from the city sounded really nice."

His eyebrows raised. "*Oh*, I hear you on needing a break. In fact, that's why I moved here a year ago. Needed a break from the busy life of city living."

The bigshot from New York City was making waves in her heart with little to no effort. Her eyes locked on his, she asked, "What do you do for work?"

"I'm a day trader for the stock market. It's not the most fulfilling job in the world, but it allows me freedom to live wherever I want."

"Sounds cool."

Jacob was attractive and had an easygoing feeling about him to Natalie. She already liked him and didn't know him at all. Martin, her first husband, had a similar effect on her when they first met. Her mind stepped in and over her heart and started to coach her. *Don't instantly be attracted to him. You don't even know him!* Natalie turned toward the fence, directing her attention back to it. *You can't go for any guy who just shows you the least bit of attention. Not again . . .*

Natalie became uncomfortable with what was stirring inside her and the war that was on the verge of breaking out. She set her pliers down. Rising to her feet, she took a step back from the fence and from Jacob. "I'll let you finish up here, Jake. Seems like you know what you're doing."

"That's a stretch, but if you need or want to go, that's fine too. I can manage." He smiled, and her heart radiated warmth like a teenager interacting with a crush. *What is wrong with me?* she wondered.

Turning toward the direction of the farmhouse, she turned back to Jacob again. "I'm going to go see how my grandpa is doing and start in on dinner. Probably switch the laundry. That kind of thing."

Jacob laughed and shrugged. "Okay. Have fun with that."

A blush crawled up her neck and reddened her cheeks. Natalie turned and walked over to the truck and got in. Turning the key over, she paused and let herself drink in the view of Jacob over at the fence. His back muscles shone through the sweat-dampened shirt he was wearing. His biceps were bulging too. For a moment, she thought about being in his warm embrace, his muscles rippling just beneath his skin. Quickly, she pushed the daydream away from her thoughts. He was a stranger, and she was a desperate and lonely woman pining after the first man who spoke to her and showed her the least bit of interest.

Backing the truck away from the fence and Jacob, she

cranked the steering wheel and put it into drive. Heading back toward the farm, Natalie reminded herself of her purpose here. School and grandpa. That's all this was supposed to be about.

~

ONCE NATALIE WAS out of sight and the truck almost back to the farm, Jacob stopped working on the fence and bowed his head in prayer. "God, help me. I need You."

Jacob hadn't been tempted to fall into his old ways in a long time, and having that beautiful woman merely inches from him took every ounce of self-control he had in his body. He thought he had moved past his fleshly desires and was on a new journey of spiritual growth and experience. Natalie, though, made it abundantly clear to him that he hadn't changed. When he first caught a glimpse of her through the truck windshield as she drove to the fence, he knew he was in trouble. Her brown wavy hair bouncing, soft perfect skin, and lush lips all drew on his desire. Then when she was near him at the fence, the scent of her was intoxicating and called out to the deepest parts of his sinful flesh. When she finally left, he watched her walk away, his eyes tracing the lines of her body. He was glad when she went. It gave him the opportunity to stop sinning with his eyes and inside his heart.

"I failed, Lord." His spirit felt broken, in need of mending. Peering up at the cloudless late June sky, he lifted his hands. "Let my soul rest in You. Help my eyes to not stray. Cleanse this wicked mind of mine."

After finishing the fence, he walked back to his cabin. Deciding to go fish down at the creek, he grabbed his worms from the fridge and his pole, then headed down to his favorite spot. Baiting the hook, he dropped it into a deep part in the creek, shadowed by a willow tree, and sat down.

Glancing at the water as he could hear the babbling of the creek up a ways, he thought about God. He thought about his life. The days never stop, never cease. Nor do the rivers, streams, and creeks ever run dry. God's goodness never stops flowing either. His head hung as his heart felt weakened. "I'm sorry, Lord. Not only for what I did with my eyes but what I did with my heart. I lusted toward Natalie. And I was prideful and thought I had overcome the folly of my youth, and yet it was there all along." Sadness lowered his heart to an even more weakened state. "You're so good to me, Lord. I'm so undeserving of Your goodness and love. Thank You."

OVER DINNER that evening with her grandfather, Natalie found it refreshing when he brought up her late mother, Linda.

"I'm sure it's hard for you too, Grandpa. You just barely lost Grandma five years ago."

"It is, but I think all death feels the same to those who lose someone. You don't fully heal, but you learn to live with a hole in your life where they used to be." Clay grabbed his chest where his heart was, and he let out a long sigh. "I've lived with a hole in my heart since my sweet Rose left, and even when your mother passed, a hole was left behind. She might have been my daughter-in-law, but she was just like a daughter to me. People who haven't been through it don't understand it."

It warmed Natalie's soul to hear him speak fondly of her late mother. "And I wish people would talk about Mom more. It's like people avoid the topic because someone is dead now and assume it's a sore subject."

"Exactly." Clay nodded. "Talking about the ones we have lost helps bring us comfort because it means they aren't forgotten."

"So true!" Natalie rose from her place at the table and stacked her plate on top of her grandpa's plate. Taking the plates to the sink, she set them down in the warm soapy water and then peered out the kitchen windows toward the front yard. It was dark now, and the lamp post near the trees lining the yard was on, bugs swarming about it.

"How are you liking it so far?"

Smiling at her grandpa, she nodded. "I like it. It's nice to be back out in the country again. Reminds me of being a kid. I wonder if my treasure box is still up on the hill."

"I'm sure it is. Hey, do you think you could do something for me?"

"Of course." Natalie returned to her seat at the kitchen table and waited for her grandpa to continue.

"Do you think Jake might be willing to re-shingle the barn roof? You could help him, and I'd even pay the two of you. I have a team of people coming to take care of it next week, but I think you two could do it and it'd be cheaper. These cancer medications are just getting way too expensive. Trying to cut corners when I can."

Shaking her head with a smile on her lips, she reached out a hand and smiled. "I would love to tackle that project for you, Grandpa." She sat back as she thought about Jacob. Crossing her arms, she shook her head. "I don't know about Jake. I think I probably annoyed him today."

"Hmm." Tapping his fingers on the table, Clay appeared to think. Raising a finger, his eyebrows shot up. "Your grandmother always knew the way to a man's heart!"

"What? Through his stomach?"

"No, through his sweet tooth! Make him some cookies and give them to him. *Then* ask."

"You think that would work?"

He shrugged. "Couldn't hurt. The worst he can say is no."

"True." Tapping her chin, she began to think and even be okay with the idea of something more coming into existence between herself and Jacob. *Martin was never Godly,* she thought to herself. *But Jake is.* It brought her a measure of confidence, and so she decided she would approach him.

CHAPTER 3

*S*tepping off the treadmill in the workout room of his cabin, Jacob grabbed the towel from the weight bench and patted his forehead dry. Neither fishing nor the run helped stop the thoughts swirling in his mind. All he could think about was her. The cute new brunette next door. Prayers helped extract the lust from his thoughts of her, but Natalie still stayed stuck in his mind. He wanted to be near her, and he didn't understand why.

Exiting the room, he tossed the towel in the laundry room off the hallway and headed for the shower. Washing away the sweat, he began to pray. "God, I don't need distractions. I need You. I'm still seeking to feel like I did when I was younger and on fire for You, Lord. It's been over a year out here in the country, and I can't seem to find You. God, help me."

Turning off the shower, he dressed in a pair of jeans and a black T-shirt. Then Jacob went into the kitchen to make himself dinner. Drizzling two pieces of chicken meat with olive oil, he threw on a dash of Italian seasoning and salt and pepper and then placed them in the oven to cook. Walking over to the kitchen table, he sat down and opened his Bible. He flipped over to Psalms, the 'heart book' of the Bible. With the new neighbor weighing heavily on his mind, he knew he needed to subdue the temptation of sin wrestling in his thoughts. They threatened to take his mind down paths he didn't desire to go down. He only wanted to have eyes and a heart for the Lord, his God and Savior.

He turned to Psalm 23 and then bowed his head to pray.

"Lord . . . this woman, Natalie. She's easy on the eyes and my thoughts are clouded with images of her. My inner man desires to seek only You, but each time I close my eyes, it's her face I see. Oh, how wicked my heart is, Lord. Help me to focus only on You. Let Your will guide me. Amen."

Lifting his eyes from prayer, he read.

The Lord is my shepherd, I lack nothing.
Psalm 23:1

HE PAUSED and said the word, "Yes." He was only one verse in, and Jacob could already hear the voice of the Almighty speaking directly into his heart and into the center of his life and the issue at hand. Though Jacob had natural, normal human desires for this woman, Jacob knew deep down that he had *everything* he needed in the Lord. It wasn't a relationship with a woman that he needed more than anything in life —it was a relationship with his Creator and his Savior, Jesus Christ. He prayed.

"Teach my heart, Lord, to fully believe this Scripture. Help my soul to surrender to You, to Your truth. It's You who leads my life and tends to my every need. Not I, nor by my own power, but by Your power, God."

A knock sounded on his door, breaking Jacob's concentration and bringing his prayer to a halt. He hadn't expected anyone to visit at this hour and he raised a wondering eyebrow. Rising from his seat at the table, he swiftly moved through the kitchen and through the living room to the front door. He opened it.

Natalie was standing on the other side. Beautiful and lovely in every way, she stood in a yellow dress holding a plate covered in foil. When Jacob just stood there without saying anything for a long moment, Natalie cleared her throat.

"I made you some cookies. I feel bad about dashing off like that at the fence earlier today. Maybe we can talk? My grandfather has a request of you he wanted me to ask."

Stepping aside, Jacob let her inside. As she walked past him, he got a whiff of the scent from her hair and his heart weakened. He hadn't smelled such an inviting scent in years, and this was now the second time in one day. It was again intoxicating, seducing, and just another avenue of temptation. Lifting a prayer at that very moment, Jacob asked for the Lord's help and strength to combat the fleshly desires. *Not my will, but Your will, Lord.*

"Thanks for the cookies, but what happened earlier was fine with me. Honestly."

Natalie fell into step with Jacob and they continued through the cabin and into the kitchen. She set the plate down on the table beside the Bible and pulled the foil off to reveal homemade chocolate chip cookies. The smell of the still-warm cookies filled the room. "Those smell delicious. Thank you. So, tell me. What does Clay need?"

Taking a seat at the table, Jacob lifted a cookie from the plate and took a bite. His eyes stayed on Natalie.

"The barn's roof needs re-shingled. I told him I could probably handle it, but he was adamant that I need more help than just myself and recommended you. You don't have to do it if you don't want to. Seriously, not a big deal."

Flashes of close proximity with Natalie flashed through his mind, enticing him, calling him, and a warmth burned inside his chest as he let the images and his imagination play out fully. Calling upon the reserves deep inside of him and on the power of the Holy Spirit, Jacob took hold of each thought and forcefully brought them under the submission of Christ, stopping them. Jacob wanted to say no to the request, but in his heart, he knew that wouldn't be right. He refused to let his sinful flesh and lustful eyes stop him from serving God through showing kindness to Clay.

"I'd love to help. Name the day and time."

"I figured since you work, we can shoot for the late afternoon sometime?"

"How about four thirty?"

A knowing smile rested on her lips and she smiled. "Perfect."

Jacob's eyes fixed on her soft pink lips as she said the word. He turned his gaze away from her quickly. His sight just happened to fall directly onto the Scriptures beside the plate of cookies. He looked with loving eyes at the Word of God. *My God, my refuge, my strength,* he thought soberly.

"You a big Bible reader?"

"You could say that. I love hearing from God and that's the only place where He speaks. It's the place where I know for certain God is talking and communicating with me. I can't ever trust my heart or thoughts fully. In His Word, I find the strength and comfort I need to be sustained."

"That's a beautiful way to look at Scripture. Honestly, I don't read a whole lot of the Bible. I have that verse of the day app on my phone, though."

Jacob's lips broke into a smile. "That's only a taste of what it's like instead of a true and full drink." Upon finishing his comment, he was convicted of the pride in his heart and by the comment. He held up a hand. "I'm sorry. That was a prideful thing for me to say."

Laughing lightly, she shook her head. "Don't be so hard on yourself. It makes total sense, and I think you're right."

Natalie's eyes fixed on the Bible and she let out a longing sigh. He could see her heart open in the moment, then she spoke. "I needed to hear that, Jake. I can't expect to hear from God when I'm not even willing to listen."

Seeing his own words carry weight in Natalie's heart moved Jacob deeply and shifted his affections for her from outwardly to inwardly. In a world full of silly women and girls who don't want to grow up, Jacob never thought he'd find a woman he'd actually consider having as a wife.

Realizing his mind was running in a particular direction he wasn't ready for, he reminded himself of the truth. He knew very little about her and nothing of her past. Jacob quickly became uneasy about his growing attraction for her. He had met this woman hours ago, and here she was, moving mountains that had yet remained untouched in his heart.

He stood up, trying to indicate it was time for her to leave. He needed to end this growing attraction he was feeling.

Pausing before she stood, Natalie looked at him. "You want to start tomorrow afternoon on the roof?"

"Tomorrow is Sunday."

"That's right."

"Let's do Monday."

She stood up from the kitchen table and smiled as she looked again directly at Jacob. Her eye contact melted a part of him, and he feared the headway she was making in his heart in such a short time. *Is all I'm feeling because she's attractive?* He wondered then just how shallow he truly was. Then he thought about their conversation about the

Bible and how he felt hearing her talk about the Scriptures. *Or is there something more that is here and has the Lord's hand involved in it?* Confusion accompanied him as he led Natalie to the front door. Jacob began to regret agreeing to help with the roof. But then he recalled the ever-present truth in his life—serving others was never a bad idea.

He opened the door and she stepped out across the threshold, then as she was almost to the fence, she turned around and looked at him once more. Jacob smiled, dipped his head, and shut the door.

～

CROSSING the church's sanctuary to greet Jacob, Natalie hoped to get one-on-one time with him. She wanted to feel those butterflies again, like she did last night every time she looked at him. Not since Martin had she felt them, and for the last two years, she feared she'd never feel it again. Though Jacob worried her in a lot of ways, she couldn't help but feel drawn to him.

Tapping his shoulder, she smiled brightly as he turned toward her. He looked into her eyes and she felt that loneliness edge away from her. It was like that every time she looked at him. Her world felt okay when she peered into those endless golden-brown eyes of Jacob's, and though she knew very little about the man, she liked what little she knew.

"Good morning."

"Good morning, Jake."

"You came all the way over here to say hi to me?"

"Don't let it go to your head. Listen, you should come over and have lunch with my grandpa and me after church. I'm making tuna sandwiches."

"That's nice of you, but I have a prior engagement I cannot neglect after church today."

Natalie felt a pause in her heart. She wanted to ask him what that engagement was and with whom, but she couldn't find the courage to do so. She had known him for only a day. Spotting one of her grandfather's friends approaching her, Natalie smiled and directed her attention to the woman, shaking hands with her.

"How's your grandfather doing? You're such a sweetheart for what you're doing for Clay. Bill and I have just been so worried about him since he lost Rose. It's only been what, two years?"

"Five years. I'm just glad I can be of use to him. It's turning into quite the blessing!"

The preacher got up to the podium and the conversations around the sanctuary quieted. Natalie turned to head toward the other side of the room to rejoin her grandfather.

As Natalie walked back to the pew she had been sitting in with her grandfather, she stole a glance back toward Jacob. He was good-looking, Godly, and single. But he was thirty years old, she reminded herself. A person doesn't get to thirty years without some history. Raising an eyebrow, she began to wonder.

After church that afternoon, Natalie made herself and Clay lunch and then started in on household chores. As she cleaned, her mind ran through different back stories for Jacob. One of them being right was unlikely, but she couldn't help but focus on the mystery of his past.

That evening, she stepped outside for some fresh air and a walk. As she walked the white fence that led into the field toward Jacob's, she saw headlights flash through the trees over on his property. *He must have just gotten home,* she thought as she pulled her cell phone out to check the time. It was eight o'clock. *Where had he been?*

The following morning, Natalie drove into Spokane and to Spokane Community College. She was meeting with a counselor to go over the path she needed to take through college starting in the fall. The counselor laid out the plan she needed to take. A couple of years at the community school to fill in general credits, then she could transfer to a four-year to finish up her degree. Leaving the meeting late that morning, Natalie's future seemed bright and her spirits were up. She'd start school soon and be on the pathway toward her future.

That afternoon, while she and Clay ate lunch in the kitchen, she told him all about it.

"That's going to be great for you, Granddaughter."

"I know. I feel like I have my whole life ahead of me again. Like I'm getting another chance at things."

Clay smiled and nodded. "God's a God of second chances."

"I just never thought it was going to happen for me. I spent three years after my divorce just wondering what was going to happen and whether God was ever going to do something. Now He is."

"His timing isn't like our timing. Especially so with people nowadays. Everybody is into right now and right away. Nobody knows how to wait anymore."

Sighing, Natalie knew it was true even for herself. "It's hard to see how things are going to turn out."

"That's true, but that's what we have faith in Jesus Christ for, Granddaughter. He sees yesterday, today, and tomorrow all at one time. We can trust Him no matter what is going on in our lives. We don't need to worry. In fact, your grandmother Rose used to say that worry and anxiety about the future or our lives was a form of pride, and I believe that!"

Natalie glanced out the kitchen window and nodded lightly. Her voice lightened. "I miss her so much, Grandpa."

"So, do I, child. So do I."

When Jacob joined her at the farm later that afternoon to start the shingling project for the barn, she noticed he had a deep gouge on one of his knuckles as he inspected one of the three ladders in the lower-lofting shed, just a few feet away from the barn's entrance.

"What happened to your knuckle?"

Bringing his uninjured hand over to his knuckle, he lightly touched it, shielding it from view. Then he shook both hands away. "Nothing. Just nicked it with a knife." His eyes looked up and down the tallest aluminum ladder in the set. Then he glanced over at the pallet of shingles nearby.

"How'd that old man get these shingles out here so quickly?"

"He had a crew set to start shingling the roof on Wednesday. They dropped them off last week."

"I see." Smiling, his eyes went from the shingles to the ladder again. It was at this moment she realized he was purposely avoiding eye contact with her. "Go ahead and grab that tool belt from the shelf over by the barn's exit, and I'll grab this ladder. We should be able to get a few hours of work done today."

He went to walk, but she caught his arm, stopping him. He turned toward her.

"Hey. Did I do something to upset you?"

"What are you talking about?" Shaking his head, Jacob removed his arm from her hold and grabbed ahold of the ladder with both hands.

"You don't seem as friendly today, that's all."

His chin dipped and he let go of the ladder. Shaking his head as he turned toward her, he laughed sarcastically. "What?"

Raising both eyebrows, she crossed her arms. "Never mind."

"You've known me what? Two days? We're just neighbors."

Embarrassed by her own prying, her cheeks went crimson. "I'm sorry. I didn't mean to—"

He raised a hand. "It's fine. Let's just get to work."

The rest of that afternoon was quiet while they worked together on the barn roof. Jacob appeared to be elsewhere in his thoughts, and that loneliness Natalie had felt leave her was coming back once again. It stung like a fresh wound with salt being ground into it. It was quiet between them for the next two weeks while they worked together to complete the roof. What she had thought might be a romantic pathway toward something more hadn't turned out to be anything more than what it was—a new roof for her grandfather's barn.

CHAPTER 4

Jacob, age 22

Jacob had it all at the age of twenty-two. A wife he loved, a baby on the way, and a bright future ahead of him working at the New York Stock Exchange. He and Sandra had settled down in Larchmont, a suburb outside of New York City, just a short train ride away to the city. He worked hard during the week to provide for his growing family and he was on his way toward having a son by Christmas.

One day, after arriving home after a long day in the city, he noticed the lights in the house were off. Assuming Sandra was sleeping, as she did a lot while pregnant, he did his best to stay quiet as he put his coat and briefcase away in the closet by the front door. Making his way up to their bedroom, he found her curled up under the covers asleep, facing the window. Jacob sensed something was wrong with his wife.

Walking over to her, he touched her shoulder gently.

Sandra turned and looked at him with glossy and swollen red eyes. "I lost our baby, Jake."

Heart weak, he sat down on the edge of the bed. His thoughts spun in his mind and his heart grew heavy. "How could this happen? I thought you were far enough along that . . . ? And so suddenly?"

Lips trembling, his wife confessed that she had been hiding the bleeding from him for the last week. It was out of fear of causing him more stress than he already had with his new job in the big city. When he tried to fight against the logic she presented, he was only met with more tears, more crying.

In the days, weeks, and months that followed, Jacob came home to find Sandra in that same position in bed. Covers always over her head, sleeping, and lots of crying. He thought she just needed more time, but not even time was helping her anymore.

One day, Jacob finally caved and took his wife to the doctor for help. Her doctor prescribed her Prozac. She started on 10mgs daily, and then the doctors increased it a few weeks later. Sandra did stop crying as frequently, but there were other things that happened too. She started getting headaches and random bouts of nausea. She also lost interest in intimacy between herself and Jacob. The pills stopped the lows from happening, but they also took away the highs of life. Sandra was there physically, but with little emotion. The doctors insisted the side effects would wane with time and that they were typical when first starting these kinds of medications. After a while, though, the side effects were persistent, so they adjusted her dose and even tried various other anti-depressants. For Sandra, each change brought various side effects along with it for her. Jacob missed the happy and carefree Sandra he fell in love with, and he would do anything to help her get back to herself. The doctors told him she was special, but he already knew that.

This roller coaster went on for two years. Then in the midst of the storms of life came a parting of the clouds and a ray of hope one Saturday evening through an unexpected visitor.

Jacob's head was under the hood of his wife's car in the garage, sweat pouring from his brow. Sandra came out through the side door leading into the garage.

"Did you get garbage bags on your way home?"

Withdrawing himself from under the hood, he wiped his hands on a dirty rag as he tried to find the words to say he had forgotten.

"Wait." Sandra leaned her head out the doorway, her eyes fixed on the rag. "Is that my sunflower washcloth from the kitchen you're using?"

He let out a short breath of air, exhausted from the tip-toeing and carefulness he had to practice around her. "Yeah, I was out of rags and there was a hole in it. I figured you wouldn't mind."

"That was my mother's! How could you be so insensitive?" She slammed the garage door, and the sound sent a cringe down the length of Jacob's spine. His heart ached with a tiredness that had worn his soul down to the core. Closing his eyes, he waited, knowing she would be back in a moment.

The door opened again.

"Garbage bags?"

Opening his eyes, he squinted as he shrugged. "I'm sorry, Sandra. I forgot."

Once again, the door slammed.

Jacob blinked slowly as he went back over to the open hood of his wife's car. He thought about the fact that he had just spent all day working and now had his head under the hood, trying to fix the sound she found annoying. He wanted so desperately to find a way out of the pain and heartache of what was happening to him and to her, but he saw no hope.

He saw no future. Sandra had changed for the worst since losing their baby and taking antidepressants. Then, the storm clouds began to part.

"Hello? Is someone here?" A man's voice sounded from out in the driveway on the other side of the car.

Pulling his head out from the hood of the car, Jacob furrowed his eyebrows as he wiped his hands clean once more and walked around the side of the car. Coming into view were two people. One man appeared to be older, in his forties, and the other was a boy, fourteen or fifteen in age.

"Hi. Who are you two?" Jacob walked out to the driveway and crossed his arms.

"My name is Joe, and this is my son, Ben. We're just out sharing the love of Jesus with people and inviting them to church."

Joe handed him a pamphlet. On the front it read: **Are You A Good Person?**

"My name's Jake. I already believe in God." Jacob's comment came as he flipped through the pamphlet quickly but didn't read it. His fight with Sandra was still fresh on his heart and mind, keeping him distracted. He looked up at Joe. "What's God ever done for me, Joe? I bust my butt at work all day long and come home to a wife who doesn't care for or respect me. I don't cheat. I don't drink. I don't do anything wrong, and it's never good enough. Where's God?"

Joe nodded. "I understand more than you know. The problem with humanity is that we're all sick. We're broken and in need of a Physician. We're all S-I-N positive. God sees your work, your heart, and your loyalty. He can and does see all of it, Jake."

"Like I said, He hasn't done *anything* for me." Turning, Jacob was about to go back into the garage, but Joe spoke again.

"You say you believe in God, but I want to ask you this

question. Have you made Jesus Christ your Lord and Savior, Jake?"

Stopping, Jacob felt his heart begin to pound. He had grown up going a few times a year to church, but he wasn't ever around anyone who practiced what they preached. Turning around, he walked back over to Joe and looked at him. "What do you mean?"

"Do you have a relationship with God? Through Jesus Christ?"

Swallowing, Jacob shook his head. "I don't think so, but I'm a good person. There's nothing that I've done that God wouldn't be pleased with."

"Do you mind if I ask you a few questions to see if that's true?"

"Sure."

"Have you ever told a lie?"

Jacob furrowed his eyebrows. "Of course. Everyone has."

"Okay. So have I. I understand. Listen, what do you call someone who lies?"

"A liar." Crossing his arms, Jacob laughed and shook his head. "I get what you're doing. The ten commandments. If you're going by that, then yeah, I'm not a good person. But I can just repent and say I'm sorry."

"No. If you're in the courtroom and you tell the judge you're sorry about murdering someone, does it excuse it?"

"Well . . . no."

"Right." Joe came closer and placed a hand on Jacob's shoulder. His eyes were a soft blue, his expression communicating real and genuine concern. "Listen, God brought me to your house today, Jake. He knew you would be working on your car in the garage and that I'd be walking up the sidewalk to go back to my car. I felt a nudge to try your house once more."

"A second time?"

"We tried a couple of hours ago."

Turning his eyes toward the house, Jacob began to wonder if Sandra spoke to them. She had grown up going to church with her grandparents often. Turning his eyes back to Joe, Jacob got an idea. "Do you think God can fix my marriage?"

Smiling, Joe nodded. "Of course, He can. He can make all things new. Plus, He is the One who created marriage. You and your wife are fused together to become one flesh, according to the Bible. Can I pray for you right now, Jake?"

"Absolutely."

Hand resting on Jacob's shoulder, Joe prayed over him. From that day forward, Jacob began learning everything he could about Jesus and the Bible. With encouragement and several months of convincing, he was able to get his wife to attend the Baptist church a few blocks from their house. Jacob went forward and gave his life shortly after that meeting with Joe and Ben, but Sandra never did make the choice to give her life over to Christ. Jacob continued to become more involved with the church. Helping with the youth group, going to a men's Bible study on Saturdays, and even cutting the grass during the summer.

After a year of going to church, Jacob approached Sandra one afternoon after service. With the reality of what Scripture taught him on how to love his wife like Christ loves the church, he knew he had to be delicate about the topic he wanted to bring up to her—giving another chance at having a child.

He found her sitting in the living room, watching TV. Grabbing the remote, he shut the television off and sat down on the couch beside her. Raising her eyebrows, she looked over at him. "What is it now, *Jake*?"

He cringed at the way she spoke to him. Praying in his heart, he asked God for strength. "Listen, I want to talk to you about something. It's kind of serious." Adjusting his seat, he touched her leg gently as he peered into her eyes. He was so scared to speak about the subject. Each time he had ever brought it up, it ended with her storming off and crying. *Lord, let this time be different. Please?*

"Why do you have to be so serious and extreme? Just talk if you want to talk."

"I want to try again."

Lightly laughing, she shook her head and grabbed for the remote on the coffee table. "No." She turned the television back on and stared forward. It wasn't the typical response from the past but instead was bone-chillingly cold and uncaring. At least before, when they fought, it felt like a tug of war. This was different. It took all that Jacob had inside of his heart to keep his composure and not to let his sadness show through.

"Can we talk about why not?"

"I don't want to have a baby with you. Especially since you've been all nutty about God this last year. I don't need my child to grow up and be brainwashed by you."

"Why are you even with me?"

She glared. "Honestly? I don't even know."

Her words cut deeper than any foul-mouthed word she had ever called him over the years. Her icy condemning words tore through the layers and sliced right through the center of his heart. His eyes filled with hot tears and he stood up. Peering at Sandra, he felt regret come upon him like a tidal wave. He had married a woman who had no love in her heart, at least not anymore. Jacob didn't know if it was the anti-depressants or if her heart had just grown cold.

Turning around, he left the living room and went down the hall to their bedroom. Pulling down his Bible from the dresser, he began to read Psalms. His heart poured out through teardrops landing on the pages as he read.

O God, You are my God; I shall seek You earnestly;
My soul thirsts for You, my flesh yearns for You,
In a dry and weary land where there is no water.
Psalm 63:1

JACOB WAS in a dry and weary land where there was no water, not even a drop. His heart twisted inside his chest knowing his wife had no desire or love for God. It was in the following two years of their marriage that Jacob wandered continuously in a dry place in his marriage. He prayed earnestly that God would convert his wife's soul and that she might be won over and return to the love she once knew as a child, a love for Jesus Christ.

Getting off work early on a Friday afternoon, Jacob picked up a bouquet of yellow daisies at the grocery store on his way home from the train. He planned to surprise Sandra by being home early and sweep her away up to Montauk for the weekend to celebrate five years of marriage.

Opening the front door of his house, he walked in to find a note on the kitchen table. Setting the flowers down beside it, he lifted the note and read it.

DEAR JAKE,

I am leaving. You don't make me happy anymore and I can't live like this. I have most of my stuff packed. I'll be by to pick it up when you're at work on Monday.

~ Sandra

. . .

THE BEDROOM DOOR opened down the hallway and out came Sandra and a man behind her. Turning toward the two of them, Jacob shook his head. "What is going on, Sandra?"

"I'm sorry. You weren't supposed to be home until later." Her chin turned toward the man behind her. "He's just a friend, Jake. He's helping me move stuff out. Hey, Brian, can you give us a minute?"

Brian left out the front door and Jacob sat down in a chair at the kitchen table. Sandra pulled a chair out and sat close to Jacob, resting her hands on his knees as she tried to look him in the eyes. "It's seriously not like you think."

"You can't possibly know what I think."

"C'mon, Jake. I've been married to you for five years. I know what you're thinking about Brian."

"You're just giving up on us?"

"We had a good run, but things just aren't the way I thought they'd be. You know? When we bought this house, I was pregnant, and you'd just gotten a fancy job in the city. Things were different back then. I was different back then."

Jacob wanted to fight for his wife, but he didn't. He just sat there and let her ramble on and on about how she justified divorcing him. When she finally left with her *friend*, Jacob walked over to the kitchen sink and pulled a glass down from the cupboard. Running the faucet, he filled the glass with water and then shut it off. Walking back through his house, he stopped just shy of the coffee table in the living room. Taking a long drink of water, he suddenly threw it against the wall and at the picture frame of their marriage certificate.

The following week, Sandra followed through on her word and retrieved the rest of her belongings while he was at work in the city. A couple of months after that, they both signed on the dotted line and the marriage was over. The house was sold for much more than they had originally paid for it five years ago. With his share of the money, Jacob was able to move to the city to be closer to the exchange. He lived in an apartment for the following two years while he stayed working at the New York Stock Exchange. He worked long hours and started missing church. He started going out to the bars with his co-workers and then he started falling into his old ways.

One early morning, he awoke after blacking out the night before. It took him thirty minutes to make it out of the woman's apartment and down a street to a convenience store to realize he was in Connecticut, a whole state away. Raking his hand through his hair as a bout of nausea broke through his thoughts, he staggered out the doors of the store and puked into a garbage can outside. Shaking his head, his eyes filled with hot tears. *What am I doing?* he thought to himself. Stumbling over to an alley on the side of the building, he pressed a hand against the red brick wall to balance himself.

"You don't look so hot, Gringo."

Lifting his eyes, he saw three men approaching, all Hispanic and covered in tattoos. He panicked and turned to run but fell. Blood oozing from his lip, he feared for his life. The three men came to him and helped him to his feet. Dusting him off, the one guy who looked rougher than the rest smiled at him.

"You know what you need, homie?"

Jacob's eyes widened and he shrugged.

"You need some Jesus."

That morning, in a little town north of the Connecticut and New York border, Jacob rededicated himself to Jesus Christ and never looked back again.

CHAPTER 5

*R*ising early Tuesday morning from his bed, Jacob slipped on a pair of jeans and pulled a hoodie over his head to go meet his friend Andrew for a cup of coffee. It was a weekly get-together after meeting Andrew at a men's conference three months ago at Pines Baptist Church in Spokane. He saw a younger version of himself in Andrew. Just like when he was married to Sandra, Andrew was in the throes of marital struggle and difficulty.

Meeting at Starbucks, they each got their coffees and sat down at a table. They talked about work and God and then Jacob steered the conversation to the painful spot.

"How are things at home, brother?"

"They're rough, man." Rubbing the corner of his coffee cup, Andrew shook his head and brought his cup to his lips for a drink. "I just want to leave and be done with it all. It's too hard."

"But that's not going to honor God in the process. You and I both know that."

Andrew clenched his jaw as he glanced away from Jacob. "I know. It's just hard. She's insufferable."

"You have to love her the way Christ loves the church, brother. I remember I used to think about how Jesus loves me despite how messed up I was. In fact, I still have to think that way. Andrew, I've done things that I'm too embarrassed to admit to you. I've done evil at times in my past. But we can go to our Creator and our Redeemer, Jesus Christ. It's He who washes us clean. It's His blood that has cleansed our dirty souls."

"But if I can figure out she's cheating on me . . . I can leave her, right?"

Swallowing a drink of his coffee, Jacob looked squarely into his friend's eyes. "In the beginning, it was not so."

"What?"

Pulling his Bible over to him, Jacob looked up the Scripture that had pressed against his mind in the moment. Clearing his throat, he read aloud.

Jesus then left that place and went into the region of Judea and across the Jordan. Again crowds of people came to him, and as was his custom, he taught them.
Some Pharisees came and tested him by asking, "Is it lawful for a man to divorce his wife?"
"What did Moses command you?" he replied.
They said, "Moses permitted a man to write a certificate of divorce and send her away."
"It was because your hearts were hard that Moses wrote you this law," Jesus replied. "But at the beginning of creation God 'made them male and female.' 'For this reason a man will leave his father and mother and be united to his wife, and the two will become one flesh.' So they are no longer two, but one flesh. Therefore what God has joined together, let no one separate."
Mark 10:1-9

After Jacob read the Scripture, he lifted his gaze to meet his friend's eyes. "You see, brother? Moses permitted it, but it was because of the hardness of their hearts."

"Right, so we can divorce if I have a hard heart."

Jacob nodded. "Technically. Listen, I'm not saying stay or don't stay with your wife if she cheats on you. Instead of focusing on what she can do to get you out of the marriage, focus on loving her in a Biblical way, no matter what."

"You haven't met her, man. She's rough around the edges. You know what I mean?"

Memories flooded into Jacob's mind of his own battles in the home with Sandra years ago. He shook his head. "Focus on *loving her*. It's not about her as much as it's about you, Andrew. Your heart. You and your relationship with God. He has given us a blueprint on how to live out our faith. This blueprint is the life of Jesus Christ. Look at the Scripture again." He pointed to Jesus's reply in verse three, and then in verse five. "Jesus points to God with His reply and He quotes Scripture from Genesis. That's how we should be living as Christians, brother. We shouldn't be walking around, airing our thoughts and feelings about every little thing, but instead pointing people to the truth, to the Word of God and to Jesus Christ, our Lord and Savior. Loving your wife like Jesus loves the church means loving her in her imperfections."

"I never thought of it like that, man."

"I want to challenge you to think of three new things about your wife each day that you are thankful for. Dwell on these positive notes instead of the negative ones."

"Will do." Taking a drink of his coffee, Andrew raised an eyebrow as his gaze landed on Jacob's hand. "Your cut's healing up. How'd you get that again?"

"Paring knife at the homeless shelter. Why?"

Andrew started laughing and nodded his head. "I just can't believe you cut yourself that deeply with a paring knife. That was what? Two and a half weeks ago."

"Yeah, yeah. I know. It was a freak accident." Resting his back against his chair, Jacob glanced over as a couple walked over and sat down at a table.

Andrew leaned in and raised his eyebrows. "How are you and that girl next door? What's her name?"

"Natalie, and we're just friends. Barely that. I haven't seen her much since we finished the barn roof."

"That's too bad. You were really digging on her."

Looking over at Andrew, Jacob raised an eyebrow. "It was lust, and I tried the marriage thing, Andrew. It didn't work out. Now it's about finding God and growing closer in a relationship with Him. I don't need a distraction."

Andrew tilted his head to the left and then to the right. "That might be, but if you believe all this stuff you're telling me about loving my wife like the church, wouldn't you experience God more if you had a wife to love like the church?"

Jacob's mind let the thought filter through. Did Andrew have a point? Could he be missing out on experiencing a part of God by being unmarried? While Jacob knew that there were plenty of people of faith who didn't marry in the Bible, he did wonder if there was some bit of truth to Andrew's comment for himself. It wasn't like time was helping to dampen his desires for Natalie in the slightest. He still thought about her daily, and the desire for her was still burning hot within his heart.

He shook his head, scrambling for answers that were comfortable to respond with to Andrew. "It's better not to marry. To live a life devoted to God."

Sandra pressed against Jacob's thoughts and his heart began to race. He couldn't do it again. The risk of being trapped with a woman who went from loving to hate-filled wasn't a chance he wanted to take.

Andrew dipped his eyes and connected with Jacob's gaze. "You sure you're not just scared?"

"Maybe I am, a little."

Sitting back in his chair, Andrew raised his eyebrows as he looked into Jacob's eyes. "Then you're not trusting God. Right? That's what you tell me!"

Convicted by his friend's words, which were his own, he smiled. "Using my own words against me."

They both laughed.

Taking a long and final drink of his coffee, Jacob set his cup down on the table. "Worry is a lack of trust, and I think you might be dead on, brother. I fear and worry I could just repeat my past."

"Listen, I know I might not be the greatest one for advice, but let me say something. You can be careful with it all. You know? It's not like you have to marry her tomorrow. If you let this woman, whom, let me remind you, is the first one you've had feelings for in years, slip between your fingers and out of your life, you could be making the biggest mistake of your life."

"You're right, my friend. Because what good is it to love the life that God has blessed me with and not share it with another? To never have children, to never have a family and to forever be alone? Then again . . . taking risks can be dangerous, Andrew."

"Sure, but not taking risks can be even more dangerous."

"Amen."

HELPING her grandfather walk the sidewalk to go inside after his trip to town for a doctor visit, Natalie was bordering on exhaustion. Holding up a good portion of his body weight on her shoulders was pulling out what little strength she had left. She had been up half the night doing laundry after he woke in the middle of the night ill. Trips to the doctor were beginning to take a real toll on Clay's body. She had called her dad while Clay was in his appointment earlier that day, but her father hadn't answered. Finally, with Clay in his bed, she exited his room and quietly shut the door.

Breathing a sigh of relief, she went into the kitchen to find a full sink of dishes. Her eyes watered. *It wasn't supposed to be this difficult,* she thought as she wiped her eyes and went over to the sink. Filling one side of the sink up with hot soapy water, she moved the dishes into the water, leaving the ones that wouldn't fit on the counter beside the sink. As the steam lifted off the water, it caught rays of sunshine beaming in through the windows in the kitchen. Her heart longed for God to comfort her aching heart. *You see what I'm dealing with here, Lord. Right? Can you bring me some sort of relief? I still haven't started school yet and I . . . I just feel like I can't get ahead taking care of him. Help me, please.*

Sliding her hands into the hot water, she welcomed the heat against her skin. Her fingers danced along the plates in search of the washcloth. Natalie located it inside a cup. She began to wash the dishes. As she washed, the rays of sunshine coming from outside caught her eyes. She then realized in that moment that God *does* in fact see her, and He sees it *all.* Her heart and lips broke into a smile as she felt loved by God.

Halfway through with cleaning the dishes, her cell phone rang in her back pocket. Rinsing her hands, she wiped her hands on the hand towel hanging from the stove and answered.

It was her dad.

"Sorry about that, was in a meeting earlier. What's up?"

"I'm getting a little exhausted out here. He is getting

weaker and things are tough." Glancing out from the kitchen doorway to make sure he wasn't in earshot, she lowered her voice as she continued. "Like, for instance, bathing. Do you know how disturbing that whole process is?"

"I didn't even think about that. Hmm." Her dad was quiet for a moment. "Why don't you let me have a nurse come out and take care of the bathing part of things? Would that help?"

"Yes. That could help. Dad . . . I really don't think he cares that I'm here. You sure you don't just want a nurse full-time out here?"

"He does care, dear. He was just telling me the other night how lovely it's been having you out there. You're doing a good thing whether you know it or not."

"Okay."

Hanging up with her father, Natalie slipped her cell phone back into her pocket and breathed a sigh of relief as she returned to the dishes. At least someone else would be able to handle the sponge baths from now on. With his getting ill a lot more, the baths were being needed more frequently.

After the dishes, she tossed in a load of laundry and then went out to the barn. She needed to move hay from the upper loft of the barn down to the ground level for easier access in the mornings when she needed to feed Betsy and the other cows. Climbing a ladder inside, she arrived in the loft and went over to the stacks of hay bales. Smokey came up beside her, rubbing against her leg before taking after what she assumed was a mouse. Laughing to herself, Natalie could tell Smokey would never want to leave the farm. Grabbing one of the bales by the strings, she shimmied it off the top and then dragged it over to the edge of the loft's floor. Tossing it over, she watched as it fell to the straw-covered bottom of the barn's floor. She did this several times.

Sweat layering her forehead, it was about three o'clock

that afternoon when Natalie walked out of the barn. She was looking forward to a tall glass of ice water and a sit down in the shade after the back-breaking work of moving all that hay. As she crossed by the garage and her feet came onto the sidewalk path leading to the farmhouse, she spotted Jacob walking across the field toward the fence that lined her grandfather's yard. Thirsty, she continued inside for water.

After checking on Clay and getting her glass of water, she returned outside to find no sign of Jacob. He wasn't in the field anymore and he wasn't in the yard either. Natalie tried to push it aside as she hadn't spoken to him much since the barn roof. Sitting in the shade of the oak tree, she did her best to enjoy her glass of ice water. Her thoughts kept drifting back to Jacob. *What was he doing? Why'd he change his mind?* An hour passed and Natalie's curiosity brought her to her feet and over to the fence. Peering toward Jacob's property, she cupped a hand over her eyes. She felt the need to know what he was up to.

Jumping the fence, she journeyed through the field toward Jacob's property. As she walked, she noticed the trees dotting the hillside to her left in the distance. She still hadn't been on the hill since she arrived nearly a month ago. Memories of the hill filled the reservoirs of her mind as she remembered her childhood. Natalie used to play with Gwen and their cousins up on the hill. She thought about the hidden treasure once again. It wasn't anything more than an old metal lunch box, but it was special. *I wonder if it's still up there.*

Once at Jacob's fence, she noticed he was outside, chopping wood. Hopping the fence, she went over to him. A stacked pile of wood sat beneath a metal shelter. She watched for a moment as he set up a new log on a cutting block. His arm stretched out, moistened with sweat as his biceps bulged, and he set the log down. Then, he brought the axe around, his back muscles flexing as he brought the head into the top of the wood, splitting it.

"Jake."

Turning toward her, he tossed the axe to the ground and walked over. Wiping the sweat of his brow on his arm, his lips curled into a smile.

"Hey, Natalie. What's up?"

"I saw you walking toward the farm earlier, but when I came back out, you were gone. Did you need something?"

His chin dipped, appearing embarrassed. "You saw me?"

"I did. I just needed a drink of water after moving a bunch of hay from the upper loft of the barn. Is everything okay?"

"Yeah." He rubbed the back of his neck. He appeared apprehensive to speak. It didn't seem like Jacob at all to her. He seemed different. "I meet with a friend named Andrew every Tuesday, and this morning, we were talking about you and . . ."

Natalie's heart fluttered. Jacob had been speaking to someone else about her? She thought he had no interest in her after the roof project for her grandfather, which was no more than a labor-intensive two-week frustration train. "*Me?*"

"Yes, and I think I want to take you out on a date."

"You *think* you want to take me out on a date?" Before this conversation, she would've loved such a request, but the uncomfortable manner in which he asked made her extremely uncomfortable with the idea. "That sounds really nice and all, but I have my hands full right now with my grandpa, and I don't think it'd be a good idea. Plus, you don't really seem into it."

She turned to leave, but he caught her arm, stopping her. "Wait."

Raising her eyebrows, she waited for him to continue.

Her pulse notched up. Seeing his hand firmly planted on her arm sent waves of warmth lapping against her heart.

"I know that didn't come out right, and I'm sorry. Let me be honest with you. I've been hurt in the past, and I just can't help but worry. I am very interested in you. You intrigue me."

His words touched her soul in a way that soothed an anxious part of her heart that was deeply wounded by Martin. "I've been hurt too, so I understand."

"So, how about it? Please?"

"Yes. I would love to go on a date with you too." Natalie couldn't keep her smile from growing.

Jacob's lips curled into a smile. "How about tonight? I'll pick you up at seven o'clock."

"I'll be ready and looking forward to it."

CHAPTER 6

natalie, age 18

Martin and Natalie had been dating for six months. He was a business finance major in his second year of college, she a graphic design major in her first year, both attending school at Eastern Washington University. He was everything she ever dreamed for a man to be, except for his lack of belief in God. She figured that part would come around eventually, maybe after they settled down and had a couple of children, but she hoped and prayed it'd be sooner than that.

It was her and Martin's winter break and he was joining her on a trip to her maternal grandmother's house. Warm southern California was a welcome break from the chilly Eastern Washington winter, and the two of them looked forward to the beach and warmer weather. He'd not only be meeting her grandmother, Verna, but her father, Gerald, for the first time too.

"He's going to love you just as much as I do." Her words came as Martin wrung his hands during the cab ride to her grandmother's house from the airport. He was filled with worry about meeting her father. Martin confided in Natalie that if he ended up with only a sliver of the success that Gerald had in the world of business, he would be set for life. His success alone made Martin feel beyond intimidated.

"You're his youngest daughter. His baby. I just don't see him thinking I'm going to measure up. I'm a nobody, Natalie."

"Sure, but you're going places, Martin. You're in college and striving for a future. That means something."

"I guess . . ."

Once at the house, he was pulled, prodded, and hugged by all the family in attendance. Gerald and Chrissy weren't at the house yet, and it gave Martin a chance to get acquainted with everyone else in the family before the big kahuna descended on the home. Hours went by without a showing from Gerald and Chrissy, and while most of the people there had seemed to forget about it, Natalie hadn't. She kept stealing glances out the window in the living room to see if he had arrived yet. Finally, just as dinner was being dished up in the kitchen, she shot a text to her dad asking about his whereabouts.

Gerald: Just got off the airplane. Will be there soon.

"He's at the airport. On the way now." When she spoke the words, she could see Martin's face sour. "What's wrong?"

Shrugging a shoulder, he smiled. "I was just having fun and now it'll be all serious."

Laughing, she shook her head. "You don't even know my dad. It'll be great. He's great. You'll see."

A half hour later, Chrissy and Gerald arrived. Entering the front door, they joined the rest of the family in the dining room. Conversations were buzzing all around the table about current happenings in everybody's lives, and the children were staying well-behaved at their table nearby. Natalie's heart gushed as she watched Martin and her father talk like old friends throughout the evening. Business, sports, and various other topics that piqued both their interests made it abundantly clear that her boyfriend had been wrong about her father.

That evening, while Natalie and Martin brushed their teeth in the bathroom before going to their separate sleeping areas, she paused and looked over at him with a grin on her face. "See? You were wrong about my dad."

Chuckling, he nodded in agreement and then spat in the sink. "You were right. He is a pretty cool guy."

A COUPLE OF DAYS LATER, the boys headed out to go hunting in the woods on her grandmother's property while Natalie stayed back at the house to prepare pies for the evening's dessert. Her sister, Gwen, stole her away from the kitchen and away from their aunts and grandmother to talk privately with her. "Tell me. Are you thinking marriage with Martin?"

"Oh, jeez!" Covering her mouth, Natalie blushed. "Maybe a little. It's only been six months though. He's smart. He probably wants to wait."

Raising her eyebrows, Gwen appeared to be hiding something as her lips tightened. Natalie grabbed her arm, anxious to know what she knew. "Tell me what you know! You have to!"

"*Well* . . . Josey heard your boyfriend and Daddy talking on the porch last night, and he asked Dad for permission to marry you!"

Holding her hands to her chest, Natalie felt so love-struck by the romantic and old-fashioned gesture of asking her father for permission. "That's so cute!"

"Yeah, but Dad said no."

A gunshot sounded from outside, breaking their conversation. A gut-wrenching feeling twisted in Natalie's stomach, and she bolted for the door leading out into the backyard and toward the tree line. Lifting her dress, she sprinted down the steps of the porch and out to the trees. Panic-stricken and ill over the idea of her dad shooting Martin, she promised to never forgive her father if he had, in fact, shot him. Arriving at the trees, she spotted Martin walking with her dad, smiling and laughing as Martin held a quail in his hand. His gaze lifted and caught Natalie's heart. He waved her over.

She spoke to the two of them as she approached. "I'm sorry. I just heard a gunshot and worried."

Her father let out a laugh and shook his head. "What did you think we were going to do with these guns if not shoot them? Just carrying them around because they look neat?"

Martin smiled, joining her father in the laugh.

"Sorry. I'll let you men get back to it."

Natalie turned to leave, but Martin ran and caught her arm. Turning her toward him, he smiled and leaned in, kissing her. "You forgot your goodbye kiss." The 'goodbye' kiss was something that Natalie and Martin always had. They had made it up on their third date six months ago, and it stuck ever since. No matter when they would part, they'd always have their goodbye kiss.

"See you boys inside in a while."

Walking out from the trees, Natalie glanced back at the woods and thought about how wrong her heart had been. It had betrayed her into thinking the worst. It served as a good reminder not to let her heart call the shots in life. She knew her heart couldn't be relied on or trusted and that the Bible she believed in was rooted in that truth. On Christmas morning a week later, Martin proposed, and she said yes. Her father hadn't been onboard initially, just like Josey had told her sister, Gwen, but it turned out that a few more conversations between the two men resulted in an understanding. Martin promised her father that he would work hard to provide for her after college and they shook on it.

They married the following summer at Clay and Rose's farm out in Chattaroy. Natalie was nineteen years old. Her grandmother, Rose, had quiet reservations about Martin, but she'd only mentioned it once to Natalie in the time of her and Martin's courtship. After the marriage ceremony, the two newlyweds moved in together in an apartment off-campus of the college they were attending. It was hard financially, but they made it work.

Seven months later, Natalie decided to take a break from school to work full-time and take care of the bills that had been piling up. Martin stayed in school. After all, Martin had the real job potential and a job lined up. Working for her father or somewhere else, regardless, a job in business finance would make way more than a graphic designer. Her working was a short-term solution in her mind, and Martin now only had a year left until graduation. In her mind, everything would work out fine.

Graduation day came for Martin a year later, and the two of them were elated. A big celebration was in order, and her father was throwing the party for it at his house. Martin, as usual at any event, drank a lot of beer and did so early in the day. By one o'clock that afternoon, he was swimming in her father's pool and hollering at everyone to jump in with him. While Martin splashed in the pool and college friends in attendance started to jump in and join him, Natalie withdrew from the pool area and went inside. Pouring a glass of water in the kitchen, she went and sat in the living room for a moment of silence. Pressing a hand against her forehead, she felt embarrassed about how her husband's behavior had gone from okay to terrible in a short span of time.

"Hello, my child."

Looking up, she saw her grandmother Rose, and she composed herself on the couch. Straightening her back, Natalie smiled, trying to hide the pain edging in at her heart.

"I warned you about him two years ago, right before you married him, dear."

Natalie's façade fell away, the smile falling to the wayside. It was no use trying to hide the truth from her grandmother. Natalie nodded lightly and breathed a stream of air out from her lips. "He's my husband now, Grandma. What can I do?"

Smiling, Rose shrugged and sat down beside her. "You're kind of stuck with the idiot now. Is there any hope of faith in that man?"

Swallowing hard, Natalie dropped her head.

"That's what I thought." Rose turned her head, glancing at her husband, Clay, just outside the sliding glass doors on the patio. A smile grew on her lips as she studied him. "I've been married to your grandfather Clay for a very long time. I still light up when I see him. You know why that is?"

Her head turned toward Natalie, and Natalie looked over at her.

"Because he's perfect?"

Rose let out a loud laugh, shaking her head. "Oh, heavens, no! He's far, far from perfect, my child. He loves the Lord. *But* that hasn't always been the case. I've seen that man go from the chief of sinners to one who has been transformed into the image of Christ more and more with each passing day. My heart has experienced the love of God more through that man's love for me than any other person I have ever known in my life. But the point of all this is to say . . . without God at the center of your marriage, you will fail."

"But if grandpa wasn't a believer at first . . ." She shook her head, confusion filling her mind. "Then why were you so adamantly opposed to Martin?"

She leaned slightly toward Natalie. "It's not impossible for your husband to come to Jesus, but it takes a whole lot of heartache in the process and a willingness on the other party to do so. Sadly, more often than not, it just doesn't work out . . ."

Suddenly, Martin jammed open the sliding glass door and ran inside soaking wet. Slipping on the floor, his feet flew into the air and his back hit the floor hard. Cringing, Rose and Natalie just looked at each other and shook their heads.

EIGHT MONTHS POST-GRADUATION, Natalie began to get the sense Martin would never get a job. He was out nightly with friends, and he'd sleep in until noon. When she would arrive home from work, she'd find him napping on the couch or hurrying off the computer as she walked in, claiming he was just filling out applications. She suspected it wasn't that, but that he was only playing video games. So, one day, after arriving home, she saw him close the laptop lid immediately and then excuse himself to go shower. Suspicious and wondering if he was really filling out applications day after day, she sat down at the kitchen table as she heard the shower turn on. *Maybe after I catch him playing games, he'll really get a job so I can go back to school.*

Opening his browsing history, she was not only surprised but repulsed. Not only was he not applying to jobs, but he was viewing pornography. Her eyes welled with tears and she began to weep. Pressing her hand against her forehead, she prayed and cried out to the Lord. *Why am I not good enough for him, God? Why would he do this?*

Hearing the shower turn off, she lifted her moist and reddened eyes and glared toward the bathroom. She was close to hating him. Standing, she went to the bathroom. Flinging open the door, she shook her head.

"How could you, Martin?"

"What? What's going on? Can't you see I'm in the middle of getting out of the shower?"

"I saw your internet history!" Shaking her head as it felt her heart was breaking over and over, she looked him in the eyes. "Why am I not good enough for you?"

Martin shook his head and furrowed his eyebrows. "How dare you invade my privacy."

"What? Are you *serious* right now?"

His jaw clenched and he nodded. "Yeah! I am! What I do on my personal laptop is none of your business."

"Yeah, sure. You also aren't looking for a job! You're cheating on me and not looking for jobs. Yay! I hit the jackpot with you!"

Furious, she left the bathroom, more tears streaming down her cheeks, and she went into the bedroom. Sitting on the edge of her bed, her broken spirit bowed her head and she prayed. *I feel so alone right now, God. Where are you? What have I done by marrying this man? How could I have been so dumb?*

The bedroom door opened a few moments later, Martin standing in the doorway. Natalie looked over at him, wiping tears from her eyes.

"Oh, c'mon! Give me a break, *Natalie.* I'll get a job."

"What about the pornography?"

He let out a sardonic laugh as he went over to the dresser and retrieved clothing. "Sure. Whatever. I won't look at it. *I swear . . . you're such a prude, thanks to your belief in God.*"

Natalie had random bouts of sadness throughout their relationship, but in that moment, something deep inside her changed. It was as if Martin had kicked her off a cliff, letting her fall backward into a sea of numbness. The blinders fell away from her eyes and the scales were removed. She knew in that moment that Martin would never change. Isolated, trapped, and knowing that he'd one day leave her, she resolved in her heart and mind to do her best to love him while she waited for her rescue from above.

One year into his unemployment post-schooling, and three years into their marriage, Martin arrived home from a ski trip that he had taken with his friends.

He tossed his duffel bag on the couch as he shut the apartment door. "I have great news."

"One of your friends got you a job?" Natalie smiled warmly as she handed him a cup of cocoa. "Or wait, maybe you decided to work for my dad?"

"*No.* I've decided I want to go back to school and get a degree in advertising."

Her heart sank. "But I am going back when you finally find a job. Remember? The plan was for you to graduate and get a job, then I can go back to school."

Shaking his head, he came closer and set the cocoa down on the dining room table. Grabbing her arms gently, he smiled. "I liked business, but I *love* advertising. Kyle was telling me that advertising is where the money is. It's going to be great!"

He pulled his cell phone out to go tell his parents and Natalie retreated to her bedroom to cry in private. That small flame of hope that he would find a job so she could return to school went out. What was she going to do now?

Natalie had resolved that the best thing she could do was to support her husband, no matter what, and stick by his side. And that's what she did for the next two years as he pursued a degree in advertising. Working at a call center for Vitamin D supplements wasn't great, but she knew she was helping Martin and their future. Tucking away a little each paycheck for a house one day reminded her that she had purpose and direction in her life. He needed his wife to be by his side and that's what she was doing. One day, the call center's call volume was low, and they asked for volunteers to leave. Knowing that Martin would be home, she took the opportunity to leave work early to spend time with him.

Upon opening the door of the apartment, she found her husband with his laptop open on the couch beside him. Clenching her eyes shut, she backed out of the apartment door and shut it. *He's still . . .* The sobering reality in front of her crushed her heart into pieces.

The apartment door opened.

"What are you doing here?"

Raising her moistened eyes, she shook her head. "I got off early."

He swallowed hard and sighed. "You should've called, Natalie."

Pushing past him, Natalie felt anger boil up inside of her. "Why should I have to call? Do you need a warning so you can shut off your porn, Martin?"

"No, I just . . ."

Slamming her purse on the counter in the kitchen, she caught his attention. Martin's eyes widened as they fixed on her.

"I want to do marriage counseling." Glancing at the laptop, she shook her head as she continued. "This is out of control. You convinced me that it wasn't a big deal last time, and that you'd quit, but you didn't. This is a problem."

"Okay. I'll do it."

And just like that, a flame of hope burned again in Natalie's heart. *This could work,* she thought in the days and weeks that followed. Things did work. They even got better. Martin stopped viewing pornography and even dropped out of his pursuit of an advertising degree to get a job with his business degree. Natalie didn't go back to school, though. Not yet. Martin wanted both of them working to save up for their house together in which they'd raise a family.

~

AFTER SIX YEARS of marriage and three years of saving for a house, they had enough for a generous down payment. Natalie had been daydreaming of the perfect house to start their family in. She kept telling herself the next chapter of their life was starting and it was time to start reading books on parenting and motherhood. She collected every book she could find on the topic.

One Thursday afternoon, while she was sitting at home reading a home decorating magazine on her day off, she could hear light conversation outside the front door. Closing her magazine, she could hear the door unlock and then her husband's voice. Following his voice was a woman talking.

Rising to her feet, Natalie stared toward the door as it opened fully.

Then, Martin and a woman in a red dress came into view.

"What are you doing here?" His face reddened. The woman behind him frowned and hid behind his shoulder.

Eyes welling with tears, Natalie looked directly into his eyes. Her voice cracked. "Who is that?"

"Veronica." He puffed out his chest and declared, "We're in love."

Blinking slowly, Natalie's gaze landed over at the magazine about motherhood on the couch. Almost able to see the magazine burst into flames within her mind, her eyes released the hot tears. She remembered Martin's history with porn. *Is this the natural next step for him?* She wondered as he ushered Veronica out of the apartment. He shut the door.

Natalie sat down on the couch. Everything was numb, including her heart.

"Listen, I know this probably seems confusing, but I can explain everything." Martin sat down beside her.

"We're in the middle of buying a house, Martin." Pressing a hand against her forehead, she shook her head. *"I've wasted so much of my life on you."*

"Look, I didn't mean to fall in love with Veronica. We met at my *job*. Remember? You wanted me to get a job."

"Yes, this is my fault. Right, Martin?"

He got up and stormed to the bedroom. She could hear him cursing as he packed his belongings in a duffel bag. As he gathered his things, a part of Natalie was relieved. At least he didn't wait until they bought a house. At least he didn't wait until they were three kids in and had a dog. As Martin grabbed the front door to leave, Natalie finally rose from the couch.

"Martin?"

He paused, turning toward her. "Yeah?"

"Don't forget." Crossing the living room over to him, she leaned in and kissed his cheek. "Our goodbye kiss. Goodbye forever, Martin."

CHAPTER 7

*D*riving over the bridge and up to the trees lining the front yard, Jacob parked his car and got out. As he walked the path leading to the farmhouse, he peered up to the clouds as he prayed for his first date with Natalie to go well. He hadn't been on a date since he had dated his wife, Sandra, nearly ten years ago.

Before he could reach the door off the porch, Natalie emerged through the doorway wearing a blue dress, her hair curled, and a smile that could steal any man's heart rested on her perfect pink lips. Jacob's heart raced as his eyes drank in her beauty.

"You look radiant, Natalie."

A light blush reddened her cheeks. "Thank you."

Turning on the path, they fell into step together back toward his car. "What have you been up to since I saw you?"

"Finished cutting firewood, did some laundry, and meal prepped a little bit for the week."

"Meal prep?" Natalie's voice heightened as she raised an eyebrow. "I didn't peg you as a meal prep kind of person, although now that I think about it, that does explain your extreme reaction to Betsy eating your garden."

"Ha! Yeah . . . I am glad we fixed that fence. What kind of guy did you peg me for?"

She smiled.

As they arrived at the car, he opened the door for her, letting her get in first. As she got in, a whiff of her scent caught his nostrils and he glanced upward again at the clouds. *Lord, let my thoughts be pure with this woman.* Shutting the door, he rounded the front of the car and got in.

As he drove, he kept asking questions about Natalie. He wanted to learn about her heart, about what made her tick. Simple things like favorite smells and flavors of ice cream filled much of their conversation on the car ride. Then, as dinner got underway, it turned more serious in nature.

"What's the most serious relationship you've had?"

Pause filled her in the moment. Jacob studied her. She appeared uncomfortable, quickly grabbing her glass of ice water from near her plate. Seeing that she was uneasy, he took the lead.

"I'll go first. I was married."

Her eyes widened and she immediately set her glass of water down. "How long?"

"Five years."

"Six here." Natalie loosened up, appearing to relax in her seat at the table. "I had no idea you were married before, Jake."

"Me neither about you." Jacob thought about the struggles he had endured with Sandra for a moment, a million memories filing through his mind in an instant. Then he thought about that final day, when Sandra and *Brian* had come by the house. He shook his head, shaking off the part of his past he had hoped to forget. "Divorce is hard. The Bible describes marriage as two becoming one, and it is like that. Two pieces

66

of wood glued together to become one singular piece. Divorce is the ripping apart of those two fused pieces of wood."

"Lots of splinters, that's for sure." Natalie looked away for a moment, appearing to be deep in thought for a moment's time. Her voice grew somber, pain resting in her tone. "Why couldn't God have prevented me from going down that path from the start with Martin?"

Hearing God be brought into the conversation warmed Jacob's heart and grew his attraction toward her. He leaned in slightly. "God doesn't want to control us. He wants our hearts. He isn't going to prevent us from making mistakes. In fact, if it wasn't for my marriage and the struggle I had endured, I know my faith wouldn't be where it's at today, if in existence at all."

She smiled and nodded in agreement. "I concur. He's the one who placed the forbidden tree in the garden of Eden. We have to have a choice. It just seems like there should be an easier way to do life."

"Oh, there is, but a lot of times, we're too dumb to figure it out, including myself. The Bible is the answer to how to do life. If a young person lives by the Scriptures and relies on God, they won't be perfect and immune to sin, but they won't make as many dumb choices. I know if I had faith back in the day, my life wouldn't have gone so far south like it did." He thought about his rough days after the divorce and the slide he experienced even after coming to faith. "Even with faith and Jesus, we make mistakes." Pausing, his heart felt weakened by the memories of his wrongdoings. Then, he thought of Jesus and smiled. "Thankfully, we have Jesus. He's paid the price for all the wrong we've done. He's provided us freedom from sin, and ultimately, we can't let the past control us."

Natalie's somber expression turned into a smile. "Amen."

Her eyes fixed on Jacob's and flickered in the light of the candle on their table. "I like that—*'We can't let the past control us.'*"

The two hearts continued their evening with a newfound connection they hadn't previously known. It was as if God had brought them together for a reason. Jacob smiled at the thought of it. And though Jacob didn't know the details surrounding Natalie's divorce and all of her past, he was able to enjoy his time with her.

Back at the farm that evening, the two of them walked beneath the starry night sky up the path toward the farmhouse. Conversation flowed with ease all through their time together, and it felt as if he had always known her in some strange way. As the last few steps were in motion toward the porch, Jacob's pulse raced. He didn't want the evening to end, not yet.

"Do you *have* to go to sleep?"

Pausing, she turned toward him on the sidewalk and shrugged a shoulder. "I don't *have* to. Why? What'd you have in mind?"

His insides warmed as he could see she mirrored his feelings. "I have a projector back at the cabin. I could put up a sheet outside, and we could watch a movie. Honestly, I just don't want this night to end."

"I don't want it to end either. But I do have one request."

"Yeah? What's that?"

"Let me meet you over at your place in a few? I need to check in on Clay and then get into something a little cozier than a dress and heels, if you don't mind."

Jacob smiled. "I don't mind at all. See you shortly."

Once Natalie had vanished inside the farmhouse, Jacob turned around and skipped back to his car. His heart was full.

Natalie jumped the fence and headed through the field toward Jacob's property. She was wearing a pair of her favorite jeans and a hooded sweatshirt. She could spot a small campfire set up in his front yard. *Fire and a movie?* she wondered as she came closer. Coming to the fence line, she noticed Jacob, but also another person sitting in a camping chair near the fire.

"Hi, Natalie." Jacob stood up and traversed through the yard toward her. As he arrived at her, he turned to view the man sitting in one of his chairs. "That's Andrew. He needed a shoulder tonight. I hope you don't mind his invading our evening."

"No, that's totally fine." Approaching Andrew, she smiled and stuck out a hand as he stood up. "I've heard a lot about you. Tonight, actually."

"Same about you, but not just tonight." He smiled over at Jacob, then directed his attention back to Natalie. "All good things, I might add."

"Hey, now. That was confidential." Jacob laughed heartily and they all three walked over to the fire and sat down in chairs.

The flames licked the night sky, sending flickers of red-hot embers into the air. The heat was comforting to Natalie as the temperature had dipped significantly after the sun had gone down. Peering up at the stars, she felt like they were finally aligning for her in life after the magical evening she had with Jacob. *Thank You, Lord,* she silently prayed.

"You want to know what's going on in my marriage?" Andrew's voice pulled her down from the heavens and her gaze met his.

She shrugged. "That's okay. You don't have to."

"Marie has a trucker mouth and Sprague district type of demeanor. Anything with a pulse—"

"Andrew!" Jacob stopped him. Andrew looked startled. "Sorry, but c'mon. She doesn't need to know that. You tell me things so I can advise you with Biblical insight. But here without that, it would just be gossip. Why don't you play another song on your guitar like you were a little bit ago?"

"Okay, okay." Andrew reached to his side and pulled a guitar up into his lap. Adjusting his body, he strummed the strings. "Do you know *Oh, My Soul?*"

Natalie nodded. "I love that song."

He began to play and sing. As Andrew sang, Natalie could hear a familiar pain in his voice lacing the lyrics. She was moved with compassion. Peering over at Jacob, she saw him singing along with Andrew and she too joined in. As she sang, she thought about the fact that Jacob had been married previously and for five years. She wondered what went wrong because if she had a man like Jacob, she would have never let him go. As the main chorus came and they all lifted their voices in worship together, her heart filled as if it was touched by God. Again, peering over at Jacob, she now began to feel a longing inside her for Jacob's embrace. She imagined what his arms around her might be like, what it would feel like to have his lips against hers. Her heart melted.

Two hours went by quickly, light conversation filling the atmosphere around the campfire, and Natalie let out a yawn as she checked the time. It was getting late and she still had chores around the house to finish if she was going to stay on top of all the household duties like she had started doing.

She stood up.

"You heading out?"

"Yeah. I have an early morning."

"We boring you?" Andrew added.

Natalie laughed lightly as she shook her head, glancing over at Jacob. "Not at all. I wish I could stay."

Jacob stood up and walked over to her, glancing beyond her toward the fence lining his property. "I'll walk you to the fence."

Falling into step together, they journeyed away from the fire and the warmth. Natalie wrapped her arms around herself to keep warm. They journeyed across the yard and passed by the garden. The only thing lighting them was the moon, and it was full and brilliantly white.

"I had a wonderful time tonight, Jacob. I'm glad you asked me out."

Nodding, he smiled. "I had a good time too. Thanks for putting up with my friend's intrusion."

"Hey. You gotta be there for people."

Appreciation lit Jacob's face. "Yes, we do."

He took a step closer and embraced Natalie in a long hug. As his body pressed against hers, she felt her inner flame of desire for him fan, the heat increasing tenfold. Releasing from the hug, they separated, and she hopped the fence and walked toward the farmhouse.

"Oh, man, you got it bad for her!" Andrew laughed as his gaze stayed fixed on Jacob. He sat back down at the fire with a grin.

Jacob glanced in Natalie's direction as she was vanishing into the field. He nodded as he raised his eyebrows. "She gets it."

"Gets what?"

"What it's like to let life wring out your heart and bleed you dry of every fiber of strength in your soul."

"What are you talking about?"

"Divorce. She's been through it."

"Could have been her fault. You don't know that."

Looking over at Andrew, Jacob shook his head. He restrained his inclination to attack his friend's words. "Nah, I don't think it was her, man. Her heart is too soft, her soul too pure. I can tell that from talking to her all evening. Some guy broke her."

"You think so?"

"Yeah, I do. There's something in her eyes that speaks of a past she isn't saying much about. That's okay, though. I don't have to know everything."

Andrew laughed and clapped his hands.

"What?"

"You wouldn't even ask her out and now you're a student of this woman. Like you're going to Natalie college or something. You're just a funny dude."

"I don't date to just date. It's for the purpose of marrying, Andrew. So, becoming a 'student' is important." His eyes turned toward the direction of the farmhouse. "I pray that God directs my path and not the desires of my flesh."

"Man, your faith. It's so solid. How did you get to that?"

"I didn't do anything. God did. Lots of refinement from the Lord, and I'm not solid, Andrew. I merely understand my utter dependence on God."

The two of them continued their conversation about God, then it flowed into talk about Andrew's difficult day. Disaster had unfolded following their coffee together that morning, while the opposite happened for Jacob.

"Then I said, 'Baby, let's work on you and me,' and she started throwing out the divorce word. I was like, 'Why are you talking like that, boo?' Man, I don't know how to handle that."

"Was she upset about something?"

"Yeah, she was, but I don't want to talk about that."

"Maybe that's the problem."

Andrew nodded, pursing his lips. "You good if I stay the night here? She said don't come back."

"Yeah, brother. You are welcome here anytime."

After the fire died, Jacob and Andrew went inside the cabin. Opening the cabinet in the hallway, Jacob retrieved the extra pillow and blanket for Andrew. Walking back down the hallway, he could hear Andrew on the phone, and he paused before entering. Leaning his head against the wall, he listened.

Andrew's voice was low. "Mercedes. Listen to me. She isn't going to suspect anything about the two of us. She's too focused on me and all the stupid stuff I've done."

Jacob's heart kindled with anger. Pulling himself away from the wall, he stepped around the corner and threw the pillow and blanket off to the side.

"Who is Mercedes?"

Turning away from Jacob, Andrew said into his phone, "I gotta go." Hanging up, he stood up from the couch and held out his hands. "Listen, man, you don't understand what's going on."

"Yeah, I do. You're cheating on your wife!"

"No. Listen, she's just a friend."

Jacob held up a hand, refusing to let himself listen. "You lied to me at the campfire. You've been lying to me this entire time. Working it out was never your plan. Get out of my house now, Andrew."

"What? And go where? My wife won't let me back into the house."

"I don't care where as long as it's not here."

"Whatever, man. You're not kicking me out."

Coming around the couch, Jacob got within three inches from Andrew's face. His jaw clenched and his anger boiling over, he shook his head. "Don't test me. Get out."

"Fine."

Andrew grabbed his duffel bag and headed for the door. "I don't know what your problem is, man. She's just a friend I found after everything that was going on at home."

"It doesn't matter when or who it is. Marie is your wife and you are married. What blows my mind is the fact that you were meeting me for marriage advice."

"I was on the fence."

"About what?"

"Never mind. You don't get it. You'll never get it, *Mr. Holier-Than-Thou*."

"You're right, I don't get it. Because you're supposed to be a Christian, a follower of Jesus Christ, and love your wife!"

Andrew slammed the door behind him on his way out.

Rubbing his hand over his face, Jacob shook his head and sighed deeply. Then he picked up the pillow and blanket from the floor and headed back down the hallway to put them away. His anger still hot, he went into his bedroom and fell to his knees in prayer.

"God, I am so very angry right now. I want to murder, I want to gossip, I want to destroy! Help me get control over this wicked flesh! My feelings are too strong for me, Lord, but they are not too strong for You. Strengthen Your servant, please, Lord."

Pausing, he thought about Andrew.

He thought about Andrew's wife.

He thought about the mistress.

"You hate what is wrong, what is evil, and what is sin. I also hate these things, Lord. Let my heart love, but also let it forgive quickly because of how much You have forgiven me. Help my unintelligent friend Andrew, Lord. Help him come to the truth."

Rising to his feet, Jacob retrieved his Bible from the kitchen and took it into his bedroom. Sitting on his bed, he skimmed chapters in the book of Psalms, knowing he'd find something to relate to his heart.

> *Do not fret because of those who are evil*
> *or be envious of those who do wrong;*
> *for like the grass they will soon wither,*
> *like green plants they will soon die away.*
> Psalm 37:1-2

PAUSING, Jacob let the Scriptures break through the walls of his heart and minister to his inner being. He knew his own fretting was wrong. Reading the second verse again, he was reminded of God's sovereignty and timing. It was the Lord and His perfect timing that held all things together. While his friend Andrew had done an evil thing by being with a woman not his wife, deep down, Jacob knew the truth about sin. It would run its course and it would lead to death. He continued reading.

> *Trust in the Lord and do good;*
> *dwell in the land and enjoy safe pasture.*
> *Take delight in the Lord,*
> *and he will give you the desires of your heart.*
> Psalm 37:3-4

PAUSING, he prayed. "Help me to trust in You." Though it felt to Jacob as if his entire life was now devoted to trusting God and doing what was good, tonight proved he still lacked a measure of trust. His emotions wouldn't have run as wildly if he had a handle on them. "Forgive me, Lord." Jacob was so adamant about doing good, he would even return a shopping cart all the way back inside a grocery store if the cart return was full. His desire was always to please the Lord with each day and each action, but he knew no matter how much good he did, there was always room to grow. As Jacob re-read verse four, his heart was filled with joy as one thing came into view when he thought about the desire of his own heart —Natalie. He had enjoyed the time he spent with her on their date, but there was one problem. He had become so overwhelmed with the revelation about Andrew that he hadn't taken the time to even bask in how glorious the date had been. Heart weakening, Jacob's eyes moistened. He bowed his head.

"Lord . . . I have prayed for a woman like Natalie for years. It all started after I found you, Jesus. I wanted that woman to be Sandra. Now You have answered Your servant's prayer, but the enemy, the Devil, has sent a distraction my way. Let my heart and mind not be distracted by the tactics of the enemy. Thank You for the time tonight I spent with a Godly woman. Lord, I pray that Your will be done in regard to her and myself. If that means she's not the one, let me know quickly and be freed of my desires for her. If she is the one You want me to be with, please let me know and make it abundantly clear."

Jacob continued reading and praying. As he came to verse eight in Psalm 37, his eyes welled with tears.

> *Refrain from anger and turn from wrath;*
> *do not fret—it leads only to evil.*
> *Psalm 37:8*

He thought about his anger that had flared tonight. His actions and words had a tendency to follow how he felt inside. "Cleanse my wicked heart, Lord! Let me be far from anger and the evil it leads to. Deliver me, Lord, and let my actions only speak of love and truth."

Wiping his eyes, he stood up from his bed and went out to the living room. Grabbing his cell phone, he called Andrew.

"What do you want?"

Jacob's heart ached as he overlooked the insult and was able to see Andrew hurting. "I don't agree with your seeing a woman outside of your wife. But if you need a place to lay your head tonight, you can come back. I won't yell, I won't scream, but I will speak the truth to you."

"All right. Thank you. I'm turning around now."

Hanging up from the call, Jacob fell to his knees. "Lord, help me."

CHAPTER 8

The nurse that Natalie's father had hired showed up for the first time the following Monday. Her name was Emily, and she had soft eyes and a gentleness to the way she spoke and interacted with Clay. For the first half hour of her time at the farm, she sat and talked with Clay. Natalie kept her distance as she watched carefully as the stranger befriended and showed kindness to him. At one point, the two of them fell into conversation about Natalie's late grandmother, Rose. Natalie's heart warmed hearing of her grandfather speak of their love to Emily.

After bathing Clay and helping him get comfortable in bed, Emily came into the kitchen. Natalie was at the table, busy reading over her class schedule that would start in three weeks' time. It looked like a rather easy load, but that wasn't necessarily a good thing to Natalie. She liked a challenge. English Composition, for instance, would only be a challenge for her when it came to staying awake for the hour inside the classroom. Regardless of the class load's relatively easy appearance, Natalie still found herself nervous.

As Emily came closer to the table, Natalie closed her laptop screen and her gaze lifted.

"Your grandfather is a sweet soul, Natalie." Taking a seat at the kitchen table, Emily clasped her hands together and raised her eyebrows. "I would like to offer some advice to you. That is, if you don't mind."

"I need all the help I can get!" Laughing lightly, she shook her head as she peered into the eyes of the help her father had hired. "What can you tell me?"

"He's getting frailer and I'm afraid he's not getting enough nutrition in his diet. I'd suggest blended foods."

"Clay won't eat blended foods. What about smoothies?"

"That's a good idea." Emily glanced over her shoulder toward the hallway leading back to her grandfather's room. "Lots of water. Keep him hydrated. Try to get him up and moving around at least once or twice a day. He has to keep moving."

Natalie's heart ached knowing that she hadn't been forcing him to move. Touching her forehead, she shook her head. "I am a terrible help."

Emily reached a hand over to touch hers. "Oh, no, dear! Don't feel bad about what you've done. Instead, just focus on the days ahead. I think you've done a great job."

"Thank you."

"Your grandfather informed me that you're going back to school. Can I ask what for?"

"To get a degree."

Emily laughed and covered her mouth. "Beg my pardon. I meant what degree are you seeking?"

"Graphic design."

"Oh, wow! That's great. What will you do with that degree?"

"There's a lot I could do. I'll have to wait and see." Her

gaze drifted to the closed laptop. "I'm nervous to go back, though. It's been so long."

"You'll do fine, my dear. I promise." Rising from her chair, Emily said her goodbyes and left. Natalie went down the hall and to her grandpa's bedroom.

Knocking lightly, she opened the door a fraction to see his big bushy eyebrows raise as he glanced over at her.

"Hi, Grandpa. You feel all fresh and clean now?"

"I sure do, Granddaughter. I love you dearly, but I prefer it this way. You know, Emily helping with the baths."

Smiling, she entered the room the rest of the way and sat down on the bed. "So do I. What do you want to have for dinner tonight?"

"Cheeseburger and fries?"

Letting out a laugh, Natalie playfully smacked him. "*Grandpa!*"

"I kid. Salmon is fine."

"All right. I'm going to have you eat in the kitchen instead of bed from now on."

"But then I can't watch my westerns."

"You need to be on your feet more. That was a suggestion from Emily. I think it's a good idea."

Clay sighed heavily. "She said that to me too. I guess she's probably right. I'll eat in the kitchen. I'm going to rest my eyes for a little now."

"Okay." Leaning over, she kissed her grandfather's head and then left the bedroom.

AFTER THE STOCK MARKET CLOSED, Jacob shut down the computers for the day and left his office, shutting the door behind him. He had made some decent trades over the course of the day and was feeling quite excited. Texting

Natalie as he heated up veggies and chicken in a skillet for a stir fry, he asked about hanging out in a little while. She replied a few minutes later saying to give her forty-five minutes to finish dinner and get her grandfather in bed.

Praying over his food, Jacob dug into his plate of sautéed chicken and veggies. Peering out of the windows that pointed toward the hills, he felt the desire to go traverse the terrain. He had yet to venture to explore that hill since he moved to Chattaroy over a year ago. *Wonder if Natalie would want to go up there?*

His affections for her were growing with each passing day. Last week's date had been the perfect kickoff. Even with the unexpected event of Andrew showing up, she kept her cool and garnered a great deal of respect from Jacob. He hadn't ever known a woman who cared both about God and him, and that fact alone about her tickled a part of his soul he hadn't known existed.

Meeting Natalie at the fence line of her grandfather's property a while later, he took her by the hand and helped her over the fence.

"Want to go for a walk on the hill? I haven't been up there yet."

Her face glowed as her gaze shifted toward the hill. "I've been wanting to go up there. I used to go up there all the time as a child. I was just thinking about the hill the other day and wondering if my treasure is still up there."

"Treasure?" Jacob grinned. "What are you talking about?"

"Just an old metal lunch box we'd stash stuff in."

"Cool. We'll have to check it out."

Crossing through the field, Jacob could see his old friend Betsy munching on a pile of hay near the watering trough just outside the barn in the field. "How's Betsy doing?"

Natalie laughed. "I think she misses your garden. I bet she won't have such a tasty garden at her new place up the road."

"Ha-ha. Very funny." He smiled, then went for Natalie's hand. As she didn't pull away but instead embraced his hand, a warmth radiated through his whole body starting in the center of his chest. Her hand was soft and delicate, reminding him of her fragile state, designed and crafted by the hands of God. Their steps continued together toward the hill.

"What's your favorite thing to do?"

Pausing as they came to the fence, she squinted and looked up as she appeared to think about it.

"I got it. Dancing in the rain."

"Oh, wow. That's cliché. Why do you like that?"

She let go of his hand, then jumped the barbed wire fence. Landing on the other side, she looked at him. "It reminds me that no matter what life throws my way, I have to be able to enjoy it. I know God is with me no matter how hard the rain is coming down in my life."

Jacob's heart and face smiled. "I like that. Another one for you. What's the hardest thing you went through?"

Jacob jumped the fence and landed on the other side. He grabbed her hand, and they started up the trail that ran alongside the hill.

"That's probably my whole marriage and divorce." Shaking her head as she let out a sigh, Natalie shook her head. "It was horrible. Hey. I want answers from you also, Jake!"

He laughed. "My favorite thing lately has been watching the sunrises out here in the country as I have my morning coffee and time with the Lord. I love it."

"And the hardest thing?"

"The divorce and marriage. Same as you. What makes you happy?"

"Right now?"

"Sure."

"You." A blush crawled up her neck and reddened her cheeks.

He squeezed her hand a little and smiled over at her. "Me too. What makes you sad?"

They walked for a while on the trail and were working their way upward toward the top of the hill. As the altitude rose beneath their feet, the farm and Jacob's property became smaller as the surrounding community came into view.

Stopping, she turned and looked him in the eyes. Sadness weighed heavily in them as hesitation lingered on her lips. "What makes me sad is thinking about the people I have lost. My mother and my grandma, in particular. On a wider scale, what makes me sad is seeing the destruction of sin running rampant in people's lives. They're miserable and they refuse to turn to Jesus."

All of Natalie's replies were working a change in Jacob's desire for her. It was changing from merely an attraction to her outward beauty into an attraction to her heart. The more he learned, the more he loved who she was as a person.

Arriving at the top of the hill a few moments later, she walked over to a tree as a breeze blew across the hilltop. Strands of her brunette hair flew freely in the wind as she bent down at her knees and began to push a rock to the side. Walking up beside her, Jacob joined her on the ground. Peering over her hands as she moved debris out of the way, he saw a faded *Hey, Arnold!* lunch box come into view.

"It's still here!" Joyfully, Natalie pulled the metal box out from the hole and unclasped the lid. Opening it, she pulled out a few shiny rocks, baseball cards, and a little heart-shaped gold locket necklace.

"What's that?" Jacob pointed to the locket.

Smiling as she popped the locket open, she turned it toward him to show Jacob the photo inside the locket. "It's my mother."

Coming in closer, he looked at the picture of her mother. "Why'd you leave it in this box?"

"I was upset, and I didn't want the reminder with me anymore."

"I hope you don't mind my asking, but what happened to your mom?"

"Cancer happened." Swiping a few tears that fell down her cheeks, she closed the locket and then put it on around her neck. "I'm sorry I'm getting emotional."

"No, don't be sorry, Nat."

Lips curling into a sad smile, she looked at him. "What'd you call me?"

"Nat. Like Natalie."

"My mother was the only other one to call me that."

"Really? With the name Natalie? Nobody else?"

Nodding, she returned the items besides the locket back into the lunch box and closed it. Then she placed it back in its place in the earth. They both stood and swiped the dirt off from their pants. "She was the only one to call me that name."

"I won't call you it then. Sorry about that."

"No. I want you to. It reminds me of her, and I like that."

"Okay."

Reaching over, she took Jacob's hand into hers. "C'mon. I'll show you my favorite climbing tree."

Following a path cut out of the tall grass atop the hill, Natalie led him. He peered over and saw two deer. He smiled. "Isn't it amazing?"

She glanced over at him, then followed his gaze to the deer who were entering a thicket of trees in the distance. "What?"

"How God made all the animals." His eyes lifted to the cloudless sky. "How He made this planet. The stars. Every-thing . . . yet He never tires. He never sleeps. He never stops being Him."

She stopped walking and turned around. Her eyes caught his. "I hadn't thought of that."

Jacob's heart filled with thankfulness and joy. "God's love for us is *everywhere* and in *everything*. Scientists, many of them, spend years searching and trying desperately to find life on other planets and yet they ignore the miracle of life that is right here on this one."

"That's so true. I love your mind, Jacob. Your passion for God."

Jacob's heart melted. "Thanks." His eyes lifted to the sky. "God's goodness never stops, and I am amazed that He even acknowledges who I am, let alone what He chose to do on the cross of Calvary. God, the Creator of the universe and everything in it, came humbly to be fully human, and fully God, and then laid down His life for us. He saved us from Hell, not only after we die, but right here and now on earth. It's the most beautiful true story in the world."

"It's weird, Jake. I've known the truth of that for so long, but I don't think about it like you do. And when I'm honest with myself, I don't think that much about the reality of what God did for me, for us. He saved us from hell, and He opened up the pathway to have a heart-to-heart relationship with us."

"I struggle too. It's hard to dwell on amazing things when they've become something we are so accustomed to in our faith. There's a beauty with taking a moment to pause. A moment to reflect on all of His goodness. He fulfills us, or better yet, He fully fills us when we gaze upon His perfect and holy attributes."

"I need to do that more."

The breeze returned, pulling her hair in front of her eyes and revealing her neckline. Jacob's desire for her burned hot in the moment as his eyes saw her neck. Releasing her hand, he took a step closer to her and slid his hand up behind her ear and into her hair. Her scent intoxicating and her pink lips only a few inches away now, he leaned in and kissed her. As his lips pressed against hers, his heart pounded harder and harder. Her taste was sweet and her touch warm as she lifted a hand to touch his arm. Feelings and emotion soon began to threaten to overtake him and he released.

"I wasn't expecting that." She smiled as she continued, "But I liked it."

"I did too." His gaze turned toward the direction they were heading on a path. "We almost to the tree?"

"Just about." She grabbed his hand once more and the two of them continued down the path.

THAT EVENING, as Natalie was reading her novel in the living room, she kept finding herself distracted, thoughts drifting back to their walk together on the hill. She smiled. Natalie could barely have a thought of him without smiling since their date just a week ago. Had God really brought a Godly man into her life who was this perfect? After all the years of pain? After all the nights she had cried herself to sleep thinking it was the end of love for her as she knew it? Setting her novel down on the coffee table, she reached for her Bible.

Opening the Word of God, she went to the book of Psalms and began to read in chapter 36. It wasn't long before she came to a verse that caused her spirit to leap inside with joy.

> *Your love, Lord, reaches to the heavens,*
> *your faithfulness to the skies.*
> *Psalm 36:5*

Pausing, she nodded as she peered up at the living room ceiling. "God, Your love for me reaches to the heavens. In my weakness and in my time of need and great selfishness, You delivered me. I was miserable in that dead-end job at the call center. You saw my pain. You saw my hurt, and You rescued me from it. I pray that Jacob and I work out, but even if that's not part of the plan You have for me, I am content. You have breathed new life into these dry bones, Lord. Thank You."

She continued reading in Psalm 36. She came to another verse that sparked pause within her.

For with you is the fountain of life;
in your light we see light.
Psalm 36:9

"Yes, Lord." She began to pray as the truth of the Scripture resonated deep within her soul. "I've been married, I've been in love, I've seen good days and bad days, and honestly, it's all nothing without You. You are the source and the fountain of life. You bring a soul joy, which no other thing can truly do. Glory to You, God! May all of my days glorify You! Your love runs deep within me. Let me not loosen from that truth. Amen."

She kept reading for the next hour. Taking time to pause and mull over each verse that popped out to her, she found herself communing with God.

Jacob hadn't been the one who had brought her this renewed joy, but he had helped encourage her in the right direction for it. Many of their conversations revolved around

God and His goodness. When Jacob spoke about God, it was in a way that brought excitement to Natalie's heart. He wasn't like the frozen chosen whom she often saw in church settings who repeated Christianese phrases and prayers that lacked life. No. Jacob's eyes would light up and his voice would fluctuate in a way that stirred her affections for the Lord deeply.

Finally finding her bed later that night, she prayed once more, thanking God for all that He had done, all that He was doing, and all that He would do.

CHAPTER 9

The three weeks Natalie had remaining leading up to her return to school went by quickly. During the day, while Jacob was working, Natalie spent her time with her grandfather and studying the Word of God. She hadn't ever read the Bible in its entirety and had set herself on an aggressive course to have it done in three months' time. When Jacob wasn't working, the two of them were spending time together and learning everything they could about each other. Natalie was finding herself falling more and more for the guy next door, and she couldn't have been happier. The Sunday afternoon prior to her first day at Spokane Community College, she ate lunch with her grandfather while Jacob tended to a friend's request at church for help moving.

As she ate her egg salad sandwich across from her grandpa at the kitchen table, she listened to him tell her another story about her grandmother and their epic love.

"I had purchased a truck on the farm account in town."

"From Steve? Your friend?" Natalie raised her eyebrows, eager for him to continue.

"Yep. Then I went and picked Rose up from her father's house and we left Plains, Montana, in our rear-view mirror and never looked back!" A worn smile rested on his lips as his aged brown eyes glowed. Love was evident in her grandpa's eyes as he turned and peered out the kitchen window. "She's been gone for five years, but it still hurts like it just happened."

"Oh, *Grandpa*." Standing up from her chair with tears welling in her eyes, Natalie came around the table and embraced him. "I love you."

"And I you, Natalie. One day soon, I'll reunite with my Rose." As Natalie went back to her seat, her grandpa raised his eyebrows. "You excited about school tomorrow?"

"I'm nervous. Twenty-eight-year-old going to college? *Ugh.*" She picked up her sandwich and took a bite out of it.

"You'll be okay. Hey. You should go up in the attic and grab the red photo album. It should be in one of the boxes with an inch of dust on top. There's a photo I want you to see."

Her interest was piqued. After finishing her food, she went upstairs and to the spare room which held a small attic door. Going inside, the attic was cramped and poorly lit, the only light source being a small window on the far side of the attic. Maneuvering across the wood beams, she found a few boxes of random stuff but no photo albums. Opening the third box, she found the red photo album and brought the entire box out of the attic and into the spare room. Lifting the photo album out, she saw an overabundant collection of letters scattered at the bottom of the box. Curious, she lifted one and peered at the date. *1948.*

Opening the letter that was addressed to her grandmother Rose by her maiden name, Brunsworth, she unfolded the letter and began to read.

. . .

Rose,

Today while tending to the chickens on the farm, one got out and Bruce got it. Mr. Skinner made me shoot Bruce. While I understand why, it pained me deeply to do it. Why can't we just fast-forward four years and be eighteen already? If only we had the ability to travel through time. Yet even if I could travel through time, I wouldn't, because that would mean less time knowing you. I love you, Rose, more than I have ever loved any other person on this earth.

She stopped reading and held the letter against her chest as she peered toward the door of the spare room. Natalie's eyes warmed with tears and her affections grew for Clay in that moment. She was in awe of the man her grandfather was and who he had become by knowing Jesus and her grandmother. Natalie hoped Jacob would eventually come to love her the way that her grandfather loved her grandma.

Leaving the spare room with the letter and photo album in her hands, she traveled downstairs and went into the living room where he was sitting in the recliner.

"Grandpa. I found a bunch of letters. I read a little bit of one of your letters you wrote to Grandma."

"Oh, yeah?" His eyes widened as he tried to see the envelope in her hand. Walking over to him the rest of the way, she handed the letter to him.

"I didn't read the entire thing. I wasn't sure if you'd be okay with that, so I stopped."

"You go ahead and read any of those letters you wish. They were from a time in my relationship with your grandma that was difficult. It took five years before we could finally get out of Plains and onward with our lives and eventually to this farm."

"You were Mr. Skinner's farmhand for five years?"

"Longer than that! I was working on his farm all the way since Mom and Pop dropped me and my sister, Leslie, off at the farm during the Great Depression in 1938. I worked for that man a long time. The last five were the hardest, while I waited to turn eighteen to marry Grandma."

"Wow. How'd you two stay so committed for that long?"

Her grandpa smiled. "*Hope*. With hope, a person can do impossible things. Eventually, your grandma used that hope to teach me about Jesus Christ and the hope we have in Him. She explained to me for the first time in my life how He is the ultimate hope for any human on earth." Opening the letter, he pulled his readers on from his neck and blinked slowly as he read over the words he had penned so long ago. "This was a hard one to write. I loved that dog, Bruce. He was a German Shepherd and I adored him. I told Rose we'd get another one someday, but we never did."

"That's sad. Maybe you can get one now?" Handing him the photo album, she stood by his side.

He laughed and shook his head. "I don't think so. There would be no point as he would outlive me and then need a new home."

She kept by his side as her grandpa flipped through the album. Stopping on a particular page, he pointed to a picture. Natalie leaned in to see. It was a black and white picture of a young woman in a dress and sweater blouse. She was holding three books in front of her and smiling.

"That was Rose at thirty-one on her first day of nursing school."

"Really? She was that old when she went? All I can remember is her being a nurse."

Clay laughed. "Well, yeah! Rose was thirty-one years old over fifty years ago!"

Smiling, Natalie studied her grandmother in the photograph.

"She's beautiful, Grandpa."

"Yep. Up until the day she died. Anyway, that was what I wanted to show you."

"Thank you. Hey, I'm going to Jake's for dinner in a little while. Do you want to join us? He said you're more than welcome."

"Oh, that's okay. I'll have leftovers from last night. You made a delightful lasagna I've been thinking about all day."

She smiled. "All right."

Jacob threw the salad mix into a large metal salad bowl, then threw in a handful of croutons and drizzled dressing across the top. Returning outside to the porch and the grill, he lifted the grill hood and took in a deep breath through his nostrils, letting the aroma of the searing seasoned meat fill his nose. Grabbing the tongs, he flipped each steak, then shut the lid and went inside.

As he walked through the living room, the front door opened. It was Natalie.

Smiling, he stopped his stride toward the kitchen and approached her.

"Hey. How are you?"

A smile curled her lips as she took a few steps toward him, sending his pulse skyrocketing. She peered into his eyes, gentleness evident in them. "I'm good *now*."

He smiled as his heart warmed at her words. "Come grab plates. We're going to eat outside at the picnic table."

Natalie followed behind Jacob as he went into the kitchen. She proceeded past him and over to the cupboard. He went to the fridge. Natalie was pulling down the plates right beside him. Opening the fridge, he pulled out a bottle of sparkling cider and shut the door. Only about a foot separated them as he turned toward her. Jacob couldn't resist. He leaned in and kissed her cheek.

She smiled at him as her piercing emerald-green eyes met his, melting his insides. "Is that all you have for me?"

Laughing, he shook his head and brought a hand up to her waist and pulled her in close. "Not at all."

Kissing her deeply, he slid his hand up her waist to her side. Jacob's heart pounded as he then brought his hand behind to the small of her back. Letting his fingertips glide across the curve of her back, his mind began going places that were not okay. Forcing himself, he let his hand fall away. In his time with Natalie, he had been learning how to maintain self-control through the power and strength of God. It required a lot of prayer and reliance on God not to give into what felt so natural. Reaching past her a moment later to grab glasses for their cider from the top shelf, he flashed a knowing smile her way. He could see the frustration in her that he had going on inside his own heart.

"You love to torture me. Don't you, Jake?"

Jacob took a step away from her and shook his head as he let out a short laugh. "Not at all, Nat. I have to be careful to not lose self-control."

Grabbing the salad bowl and forks, Jacob led the way outside. *You always provide a way to escape. Thank you, Lord.* As he stepped out of the cabin and came into the fresh air, he breathed deeply and lifted a prayer of thankfulness. After they got situated with the food at the table, she started telling him about her grandpa and grandma's relationship and the letters she had come across in the attic.

Wiping his mouth with a napkin as he listened, Jacob recalled his conversation with Clay when he mentioned

Rose. "I could tell when he was talking about her that he loved her dearly."

"He really did. Isn't it crazy they were able to wait for five years?"

Nodding, he finished his bite. "Older generations knew how to be patient. It's not like today where people throw a computer out if it takes longer than two seconds to load a web page." Taking a bite of his salad, he turned his head and admired the landscape all around them. Eventually, his gaze came back to Natalie. Swallowing his food, he smiled.

"What are you smiling about?"

"You." He opened his arms as he once more surveyed the surrounding landscape. "This. I moved across the country to find peace and solitude and to truly reconnect with God. I've enjoyed this beautiful land and everything God has designed around me, but ever since I've moved here, I have felt something was missing." Pausing, he was hesitant to continue. Continuing would make him vulnerable.

"And now?"

Pushing aside worry, he continued. "I realize now what I've been missing all along. It was you, Natalie. Not only did God create all this beauty around me, but He created *you*. A woman of God who has the tenderness of a dove, the beauty of an angel, and the elegance of a swan. I know we haven't known each other for very long, but I have to be honest with you. I've never met a woman like you before, and I don't believe I ever will again."

A blush glowed red in her cheeks. Her voice softened. "Thank you. I thought after what happened inside, you might be a little upset with me."

Shaking his head, Jacob peered into her eyes. "Our flesh may be weak, but the Spirit of God is strong. Resisting temptation and honoring God isn't easy, but they are possible."

~

Up at six the next morning, Natalie cleaned the entire house, fed and watered the cattle, and even triple-checked the breakfast and lunch meals in the fridge she had prepared for Clay. Checking her phone, she found it strange that her grandfather still wasn't up when seven thirty rolled around. Going into his bedroom, she pushed open the door and could hear him snoring. Closing the door quietly as she grinned, she went back into the kitchen and sat down at the table. Grabbing a note pad and pencil, she wrote him a note.

Grandpa,

I didn't want to wake you, but I do want to let you know you have breakfast and lunch in the fridge. Thanks again for talking to me about Grandma yesterday and showing me a picture of her on her first day. That was sweet of you. Have a great day, and I'll see you around dinner time.

Love,

Natalie

Ripping the note from the pad, she set it on the table. Grabbing her purse and backpack, she left.

When she arrived at her first class, Computer Ethics and Law, she wasn't surprised to see most of her fellow classmates were males. Spotting one of the few other women in the class, she went and sat down next to the one who seemed closer to her age than the others.

"Hi, I'm Natalie."

The lady smiled. "I'm Elise. Nice to meet you." Glancing around, Elise leaned in toward Natalie. "Is it me, or are we like the oldest people in this class?"

"Right?" Natalie agreed with a nod. "Some of the only ladies in the class too!"

"Yep."

The instructor walked in and the light conversations floating among the students went quiet. College was now officially underway.

Later that day, after her other courses that morning, she was on her way out to the parking lot to leave when she bumped into Elise.

"Hey, girl. How was your first day at school?" Elise approached, smiling.

"It was okay. I think it went well."

"You down for some coffee? I could go for a large caramel latte with an extra shot before I get home and deal with my husband and kids and a dirty house."

"I'd love that!"

Arriving at Starbucks off Market Street in Spokane, Natalie and Elise ordered coffees and then found an empty metal table outside on the patio of the coffee shop. Drinking their coffees, they discussed life, family, and love.

"You're on your way to love with that boy!" Elise flashed a warning look.

"He's older me. He's not a boy!"

Elise laughed. "A boy nevertheless!" Growing more serious in her demeanor, Elise adjusted in her chair, scooting closer to the table as she leaned in. "Keep a guard on that sweet heart of yours. It sounds like he might be the first guy you've been interested in since your failed marriage. To Martin, was it?"

It had been a long while since she had a female friend and she had ended up spilling more than a little coffee on the table that early afternoon. She told all.

"Yeah, it was Martin." Natalie took an inventory of her

heart in the moment. "But it's so different and special with Jacob."

"Give it time, girl. He's still *a man*."

"But he's Godly. Wait, do you believe in God?"

"Yeah. I believe in God." Elise held out her hands. "But what's that got to do with this?"

"It has *everything* to do with him. That's what sets him apart."

"Hmm." Elise went quiet, appearing to hold something back.

"What?"

"My papa was *a man of God* and he even was a preacher."

"But?"

"He ended up cheating on my mother and leaving her with us three kids when I was nine. I know God's real and all, but I don't think He cares about what goes on with people."

"I'm so sorry to hear that happened to you, Elise."

"Don't be sorry. I'm okay now. I have a family and I'm getting my degree. Things are looking up for me. But God had nothing to do with it. Tony's a good man, I know it. You don't know this guy Jacob enough to know whether he's a good guy or not. You've only seen what he has allowed you to see."

Natalie thought back to the roof repair of the barn. How he had refused to tell her about his coming and going and that strange cut on his knuckle. He never explained any of that to her. "I guess there are things I don't know."

"Right. With time, all will be revealed. That's the thing about these men. They can only hide behind their fake images for so long."

Feeling discouraged by her new friend, Natalie's shoulders slumped.

"Hey, girl. I'm sorry. I shouldn't go off on men like that. He could very well be a good guy. Just like Tony. I'm not trying to make you sad or anything but helping with perspective."

"I get that, and I appreciate it too. We all need friends in our life who can tell us things that are tough to hear."

"I agree."

CHAPTER 10

A month came and went with little notice. Natalie was busy with school, taking care of her grandfather, whose health was in a dramatic decline, and spending whatever little time she had with Jacob. One Thursday afternoon, in late September, just hours before her afternoon class, a car pulled into the driveway at the farm. As it passed over the bridge, Natalie sat up on her quilt she and Jacob were sharing in the front yard next to the oak tree. Cupping a hand over her eyes, she saw it was her father's Lexus. Her heart plunged into the pit of her stomach. She hadn't expected him to visit and especially didn't anticipate his meeting Jacob so soon.

Leaping to her feet, she swiped at her yellow skirt, sweeping away the crumbs from her sandwich. Jacob sat up, a confused look on his face.

"What's wrong, Nat?"

"It's my father. He's here."

Raising an eyebrow, Jacob glanced over at the sleek black luxury car as it parked. "Am I missing something?"

She shrugged.

Jacob stood up and touched her arms gently as he peered

into her eyes. "It's going to be okay. We've been dating for months. He's not a shotgun kind of guy. Right?"

Thinking back to how much her father had pined after Martin and how well they got along, she breathed a sigh of relief sensing that Jacob and he could connect just as well, especially given the fact that they share the same beliefs. "I'm sure it'll be fine. I just haven't told him about you *at all.*"

Jacob's eyes widened. "What?"

Before she had time to reply and explain that she didn't want him worried she was being distracted, her father emerged from between the trees and started down the cement path. He was wearing a pair of slacks, a white button-up shirt, blazer, and a pair of dark shades. Taking the lead, Natalie led Jacob over to meet him. Her heart pounded as they came closer.

Removing his shades, Gerald slipped them into his front blazer pocket and extended a hand. "The name's Gerald. You a friend of my daughter?"

Natalie could see a look of disappointment in Jacob's face. "Yeah. I live next door. My name is Jacob."

"Cool. Mind if I steal my daughter for a little while, Jacob?"

Holding his hands up, he took a step back. "Go ahead. I was about to head home, anyway."

As Jacob left, Natalie's heart began to pound harder as she watched him leave. She felt bad for keeping him from her dad. Looking at her father, she shook her head. "Why were you rude to him?"

"What? How was I rude? I just thought—"

"You thought wrong, Dad." Walking away from her dad, she chased after Jacob as he was arriving at the fence. Getting to him, she grabbed his shoulder, turning him around.

"Hey. I'm sorry he was rude."

"He wasn't rude. Your dad just didn't know who I was.

That's on you, not him." Jacob's glance reached back to her father, then back at her. "We've been going out for a while now. You never even mentioned my name? Seems strange."

Natalie's cheeks went crimson. It was true and it was wrong on her part. "I didn't want him to know about you because he could think I'm getting distracted. I didn't want to disappoint him or make him worry that I wasn't taking care of my grandpa."

"Fear."

"Huh?" Natalie furrowed her eyebrows as she didn't like his lack of words. "What are you saying?"

"You were operating out of a place of fear. I get it, but that doesn't make it any better. I have to go."

He turned, but she stopped him again.

"I'm truly sorry, Jake."

"It'll be fine. It just hurt a little. I'll see you around, Nat."

Turning once more, he hopped the fence and then proceeded through the field.

Walking back to her father, her shoulders felt heavy and slumped.

"You okay?"

She sighed. "Yeah, I should have told you about him."

He placed a hand on her shoulder and looked her squarely in the eyes. "Well, here's your chance."

Watching over his stocks carefully on his three-monitor computer setup back at his cabin, Jacob kept Natalie in the back of his mind. The whole experience that had just happened a few hours earlier with her dad didn't make any sense considering the closeness he had experienced with her over the last three months.

His cell phone rang. Glancing at the screen, he saw it was

his friend Andrew. His insides cringed. Andrew had left his wife and moved in with his newfound girlfriend, Mercedes, two weeks ago. He told Jacob that they were "in love" and that they were soul mates. Given everything he knew about God, about marriage, and about love and life, Jacob knew Andrew was heading down a path that was not only unwise but apart from God and sinful. Since his friend's decision to leave his wife and move in with the girl, he had stopped meeting him for coffee and created a distance between himself and Andrew.

A voicemail notification popped up on the screen a minute later. Peering once more at the stock ticker, he grabbed his cell phone from the desk and hit Play on the voicemail.

"Hey, *friend*. You have a funny way of being there for someone during a big event in their life. I thought we had a friendship, but I guess it's only when I'm doing what you tell me to do."

Heart aching, he deleted the voicemail and set the phone back down on the desk forcefully. In that moment, and in the depths of his heart, Jacob called Andrew a fool. "Lord was I ever so stupid?"

God's response, or at least that's how it felt to Jacob in the moment, was a resounding 'yes' as memories of his college days before meeting his first wife, Sandra, flashed through his mind. Girls were nothing more than notches on his dorm room's bedpost. He had slept with more women than he could even remember. He dipped his chin in shame. "God, forgive my prideful heart."

Picking up his cell phone, he longed to be there for his friend. His finger hovered above his friend's name on the screen as he contemplated. Just then, a Bible verse pressed against his mind, furthering his hesitation.

But now I am writing to you that you must not associate with
anyone who claims to be a brother or sister but is sexually immoral
or greedy,
an idolater or slanderer, a drunkard or swindler. Do not even eat
with such people.
1 Corinthians 5:11

GRABBING HIS BIBLE, Jacob wanted the context of the verse. He read 1 Corinthians 5:9-10, *'I wrote to you in my letter not to associate with sexually immoral people—not at all meaning the people of this world who are immoral, or the greedy and swindlers, or idolaters. In that case you would have to leave this world.'* The context only amplified the passage that had pressed against his spirit. *Anyone who claims to be a brother or sister . . . Do not even eat with such people.*

Peering at his friend's name on the phone, Jacob had to decide. Give into his feelings and desire to be there for his friend despite his claiming to be a Christian yet living in fornication and adultery, or follow the Scripture and command laid out in the passage. His friend's voicemail played again in his head. *I thought you were my friend . . .*

I can handle this, Jacob thought. Picking up his cell phone, he pressed the screen and dialed Andrew.

NATALIE HADN'T SEEN her dad in the same room with her grandfather in years, not since Natalie's grandmother had passed away. It softened a part of her heart to see her dad giving Grandpa a drink of water. The soft, gentle, and overall selfless side of Gerald wasn't a part she had seen much of in her lifetime.

Exiting the bedroom doorway, Natalie went into the kitchen to start on dinner. Pulling out the cutting board, she laid it on the kitchen table and peered out the windows at the front yard. Seeing the quilt still out on the grass, she thought of Jacob. Regret edged into her mind as the look of disappointment on his face came into view. She had hurt him, and it bothered her that she had done that. Here she had been holding onto worries of him hurting her, but she had been the one to inflict the hurt.

Going to the fridge, she retrieved the chicken she had pulled out that morning to thaw. Returning to the cutting board, she opened the packaging and began to trim the fat. Remembering her night class was in an hour, she hurried to get the chicken seasoned and into the oven.

On her way to go tell her dad she had to leave soon, he met her in the hallway, and he took her into the living room.

"I have school shortly, so I have to leave. The chicken is in the oven and should be done in about forty-five minutes."

"Okay. Hey, Pumpkin?"

"Oh, jeez. What do you need now, Dad?" Smiling, she was merely playing with her father.

"Come sit down on the couch."

Her father's words were weighted, and her heart raced. "What is it?"

"I just got off the phone with Grandpa's doctor's nurse. Your grandpa's last scan indicated that the cancer has spread. It's gotten a lot worse. Hospice will be coming soon, and I think it's best if you go back home."

"What?" Heart pounding, she rose to her feet. "I want to stay here."

Gerald looked toward the window that pointed toward the fence and Jacob's property. "For him, not your grandfather."

"It's not about him. I promise!" Walking over to her

father, she grabbed his hand. "I want to stay for Grandpa! I've grown to love him a lot, Dad. We are closer now than ever. I want to be here for him."

"Okay. Maybe you're right. But even that isn't a good thing. Your attachment is only going to make the process of losing him worse on you. It's going to hurt really badly, and I don't want you to get distracted from school."

Peering over her shoulder toward the hallway leading to Clay's room, her heart ached. She looked at her dad again. "Can we go for a walk? I want to talk about something with you."

"Okay?" Gerald appeared confused by his daughter's request but obliged.

They exited through the living room and out onto the porch. As they walked together beneath the large oak tree and toward the bridge, Natalie began to explain to her dad for the first time about the meaninglessness she had felt in her life prior coming to the farm. "I had no purpose or direction, and a part of me wanted to die, I hated it so much. This . . ." Her gaze jumped all around her, then came back to her dad. "This all made me realize I can do good."

Stopping, Gerald turned to his daughter with tears in his eyes. "I had no idea you were struggling."

Seeing his concern written all over his face moved a deep part of her. She nodded and then dipped her chin.

He lifted her face with his index finger and smiled. "I'm glad you found meaning out here. That does worry me, though."

"Why?"

"It's all almost over, either way. Then what?"

"Then I go back to my apartment and live my life being changed by the experience. I have already looked into what I can do at my home church in Spokane to help others. But right now? I want to be here for Grandpa the way I couldn't be for Grandma."

He smiled. "You're a sweet daughter and an amazing granddaughter." Letting out a sigh, he peered back toward the farmhouse. "You can stay."

"Thank you. Will you keep the farm?"

"No, neither Gabby nor I will keep it. Too many memories."

She noticed her father's composure didn't match what he should be feeling in the moment. Here her dad's dad was, in his final days and weeks on earth, and yet he seemed perfectly fine on the matter and was even planning to rid himself of the farm.

"Dad?"

"Yeah?"

"Are you okay?"

"Yes. Let's get back up to the house." He turned to walk back toward the house, but Natalie grabbed his arm.

"*Dad?*"

His eyes now moistened, she saw her dad in a new light.

"Talk to me."

His bottom lip slightly trembled and he shook his head. "*Please*, don't make me talk about it."

She let him go. Following a few steps behind her dad, Natalie began to pray for her father's heart. She knew he would need the strength that would follow losing his father. He had barely lost his mother just a short five years ago. Soon, he'd be an orphan, and it pained Natalie's heart to stop and think of how much pain her father was in.

A KNOCK SOUNDED at seven o'clock on Jacob's cabin door. Grabbing his television remote, he powered off the TV and went to answer the door. It was Andrew, but he didn't look good. Eyes puffy and red, it appeared his friend had been sobbing for some time. Letting him inside, Jacob immediately wrapped his arms around him in a hug, letting go of all his ill feelings toward him.

"I'm sorry, bud." Jacob patted his shoulder as he released. "I can't imagine what you're going through. It sounds rough."

"Yeah, it is. First, I leave my wife for Mercedes, then Mercedes just goes back to her baby's daddy. How could I mess up my life so bad?"

Compassion for his friend's sadness resided inside Jacob's heart, but at the same time, he knew all of sin's paths led to death. Shutting the door, he did his best to be sensitive to Andrew's situation. They sat down on the couch together in the living room. Andrew went on to explain the complexities of living with a new woman who wasn't his wife. Even though Andrew thought this was what he had wanted, he seemed to be quickly learning that this was nothing he had thought it would be. Fuse running short, Jacob shook his head as he clasped his hands, then Andrew stopped talking about his girlfriend problems. "What? I can tell you want to say something, Jake." He laughed. "Out with it, brother."

Opening his palms, Jacob searched his friend's face for sincerity. "You don't want to hear what I have to say."

"Sure, I do! Even if it's rough. Please! Tell me!"

"Your wife . . ."

"*Ugh* . . ." Andrew stood up and walked over to the bookcase on the other side of the living room. "Man, your wife cheated on you too. Isn't that right?"

"Yes. But she left me. I waited for *her* to leave."

"But my wife left three years ago!" He laughed, shaking his head. "I waited so long! Tried for so long! You know, I thought you had advice for me and Mercedes."

Jacob stood up. "You want some coffee? I can put on a half-pot for us."

"Sure."

Walking out of the living room and away from the conversation, Jacob wondered if letting his friend back into his life right now was more of a reaction with his feelings than a good decision rooted in Biblical truth. Feeling his phone vibrate in his pocket, he slipped it out and peered down at the screen. It was a text from Natalie.

Natalie: School is so boring today! I just want to leave and come see you. Can I come over after class tonight?

Smiling, he texted her back, letting her know he'd be thrilled to see her. After making coffee, he went back into the living room. He found Andrew sitting on the couch, looking at a photo album. "Who are these people?"

Jacob glanced over to see the picture. It was a picture of Joe and Ben, the father-son team that had witnessed to him about Jesus Christ all those years ago and who had become close friends to Jacob. Smiling as his heart warmed at the memory, he recapped his encounter with the door knockers.

Andrew closed the photo album and set it down on the coffee table. Relaxing into the couch cushions, he glanced over at Jacob.

"Does life ever get easy?"

"Depends how you define easy, Andrew. I think life is *manageable* when you let God lead you and guide you."

Another knock sounded on the door. Furrowing his eyebrows, Jacob stood up. "I wasn't expecting anyone else." Walking over to the door, he opened it as Andrew came up behind him.

It was a woman in a short skirt and a tube top.

"Mercedes!" Andrew hollered from behind Jacob. "You came! I thought you blew off my text message!"

∾

GRABBING a quick coffee with her friend Elise, Natalie hoped to get advice on the situation with her grandfather.

"I think you do what you think is right for you. You know? I am a big believer in just going with what works for you."

"Well, that's really helpful." Natalie laughed. "Not."

"Honestly, if you want to be there with him as he exits Earth, do it. As far as purpose and meaning in life, I feel like that's up to you. There's plenty of people who clean toilets, for example, and have a very fulfilling life. It's not always about a profession but doing meaningful things with our time, inside and outside of work."

"Yeah, I think you're right. Thank you."

She nodded and flashed a half-smile. Then she scooted closer to the table and leaned in. "How about you tell me how you and Jakey are doing?"

"Good for the most part, but I think I upset him today."

"What happened?" Elise took a sip from her coffee as she waited with eager eyes fixed on Natalie.

"*Well . . .* I hadn't told my dad about Jake. You know how that is. My dad isn't a *huge* part of my life, but I don't know, I should've told him. Anyway, he came out today for a surprise visit to the farm and Jake was over. They met, and when they did, Jake realized my dad had never heard his name before."

Elise pursed her lips. "Not good, girl. You need to apologize."

"I know. The good news is that I think he's okay."

"I'm sure he is fine, but he's probably upset. Just make sure he understands that you care about him. He's probably wondering where you guys stand if your dad didn't even know he existed. You know?"

"Yeah. I'm heading over there after this, so I'll be sure to apologize."

After their coffee, Natalie headed back out to the farm. Parking, she went inside and put her purse down on the kitchen table, then checked in on Clay. He was asleep with the old western, *Gunsmoke*, blaring on the television set. Walking into the room, she went up to the television set and shut it off.

Exiting the room, she headed outside in the setting sun and over to the fence. As she jumped the fence, she could see fire in the distance over at Jacob's property. Fear wrapped its hands around her throat and she sprinted across the field. Hitting a rock, Natalie fell and smashed her knee hard into the ground. Pushing the pain aside, she got back up and came closer to Jacob's property. She slowed her pace as the sound of music hit her ears. Classic rock. Coming even closer, she could make out an oversized bonfire in the front yard. Not a disaster.

Anger flared up inside her as she had been worried a fire had broken out. Batting it down, she reminded herself to be thankful there was no danger to Jacob. She remembered trusting her heart before with feelings when her father and Martin were out shooting quail. *Just calm down,* she thought to herself.

Coming into the yard, she saw Jacob's friend Andrew. *That's strange. I thought he separated himself from that guy.* Then she saw two scantily-clad women dancing near the bonfire. Something wasn't right and she knew it. As she came into Andrew's view, he stopped dancing and pointed to the cabin. "He's inside, napping," Andrew yelled over the music. One of the women cackled.

Flashing a fake smile, she went in the front door and shut it behind her. Jacob was indeed asleep on the couch. Three empty beer bottles sat on the coffee table near him.

Furrowing her eyebrows, she turned around and left. Natalie didn't know what to make of the situation, but right then, she remembered Elise's words to her about men. *Eventually, they reveal their true selves.* Angry and annoyed, Natalie didn't have time to play games and she definitely didn't need another Martin in her life.

CHAPTER 11

Waking the next morning in a haze and with a splitting headache, Jacob sat up on the couch. Raking a hand through his hair, he blinked his eyes as they came into focus. Beer bottles were strewn across the coffee table and seeing them ignited his anger. Piecing together last night, he recalled Andrew coming over, and then to his surprise, Mercedes. There was a faint memory of talking to Andrew and Mercedes. Then she offered him a glass of juice. Everything after that was missing. *Did she drug me?*

Rising to his feet, he went searching for Andrew. Finding his friend in his bedroom and in his bed, Jacob kicked the bed hard.

"Wake up."

When Andrew let out an exhausted groan and didn't move from under the covers, Jacob went to the side of the bed and yanked off the covers.

"Get out of my house."

Andrew let out a curse and jumped out of the bed. "What is wrong with you?"

"Your girlfriend drugged me and then you proceeded to drink and party in my house. That is what's wrong with me!"

"Dude, we were mostly outside. What's your problem right now?"

"I'm looking at my problem. Get out of here, Andrew!"

"You're a bad friend."

"Yeah, yeah. Whatever. You're an *amazing* friend yourself."

Opening the front door for Andrew to leave, he saw a smoldering bonfire in his front yard. His anger grew.

Stopping on his way out the door, Andrew turned toward Jacob. "Dude, I'm sorry. Just tell me why you are so mad. I didn't drug you, and I don't know if she did."

Grabbing hold of the upper part of the door, Jacob let his body lean on the door for support as he closed his eyes. Opening them, he peered into Andrew's gaze as he let out a sigh. "I'm disappointed in you, Andrew. But more so in myself for thinking I could trust you. I can't help you anymore. In fact, I never could help you. It was always God who could help you, and you never surrendered to Him. Neither I, nor anyone else, can make that choice for you. Goodbye."

Closing the door, he turned around and surveyed the mess. Just then, he thought about Natalie and his heart sank. "No, *Lord.* Tell me she didn't make it over last night."

Hurrying over to the coffee table, he grabbed his phone and checked the messages. She had texted him.

Natalie: On my way!

Sinking into his couch, Jacob shook his head as sadness filled him. As he began to pray and ask for God's guidance, the Bible verse that had come to his mind yesterday once more pushed against his mind, convicting him in the moment.

*But now I am writing to you that you must not associate with
anyone who claims to be a brother or sister but is sexually immoral
or greedy,
an idolater or slanderer, a drunkard or swindler. Do not even eat
with such people.*
1 Corinthians 5:11

"OH, God, what have I done? I have sinned!" Shaking his head, he prayed. "Forgive me, Lord." His thoughts drifted to Natalie once more and what she had been through the night before when she had come over. He thought about himself sleeping on the couch and the empty beer bottles all around him. He wept, and his heart weakened. "Lord, I should've listened to Your Word. Why did I fail to do so? You don't seek to control my every movement, but You instead want to lead me in the way I truly want to go! Forgive me, Lord . . ."

After a heartfelt prayer, he rose to his feet and headed outside and across the field to the farmhouse to apologize to Natalie.

Coming out onto the porch after he knocked, Natalie was in a loose-fitted sweatshirt and a pair of pajama pants. It wasn't yet eight o'clock in the morning.

"Sorry if I woke you."

She yawned. "It's fine. I have class shortly."

"I need to explain what happened last night." Jacob went on to explain all that happened. Then, he ended it with an apology. "Again, I'm so sorry for what you had to deal with last night. It was my fault."

"Yeah, it was your fault. Like you said, you let your emotions get in the way of your judgment."

"Yeah."

"Hey. So, I'm glad you came over. My grandpa is being put in hospice care next week."

Raising his eyebrows as his heart ached with pain for her, he took a step closer and touched her arm. "He's getting worse. That's sad."

Natalie took a step back and nodded, folding her arms. Wiping a stray tear, she breathed a heavy sigh. "Yeah, he is. I hope he hangs on as long as possible for my own selfish reasons, but I know he is ready and will go when it's time. Anyway, I'll be moving back home to Spokane soon after."

Furrowing his eyebrows as he worried where she was taking the conversation, Jacob shook his head. "It doesn't matter if you live in Spokane. That's barely twenty minutes away. We can still see each other. Things between us don't need to end."

"I know they don't need to end, but right now, I need to focus on my grandpa and being with him these final days of his life. You get that, right?"

"I understand." Jacob swallowed hard.

"All right. Well, I'll see you around, Jake."

"Okay." Becoming uncomfortable for the first time in their relationship, Jacob glanced away from Natalie and toward the direction of the fence and field. "I'd better get home, anyway. I'm already late with the stock markets already being open."

"Take care of yourself, Jake."

Stepping toward her, he kissed her gently. As his lips parted from hers, he looked into her eyes. Those lovely green eyes were the one place he loved to be lately. He didn't know when the next time would be that he'd see them, but he had a feeling this goodbye was for longer than she was letting on.

"Let me know if you need anything, Nat." Grabbing her hand, he gave her a light squeeze and then backed away, not wanting to let go, but she did let go.

As Jacob left the porch, Natalie's heart ached knowing that she didn't want to see him again. Her eyes watered and tears soon streamed down her cheeks. The story he had given her about his juice being drugged was too convenient. A million questions surrounded the whole situation he was in to begin with last night. Why was anyone there at all? Because he had a moment of weakness for his friend? That didn't line up with the character or 'image', as her friend Elise would say, that Jacob had been portraying to her for the last three months. So, based on that, Natalie made her decision. She couldn't let her heart and emotions call the shots. Not again. That only ended in heartache. She knew it would be a lot easier now to distance herself and cut things off than it would years down the line. She couldn't waste another seven years on a relationship with a man like Martin. Not again.

Returning inside, she shut the door.

"Was that Jake?" Her grandfather's voice sounded from the recliner in the living room.

She wiped her eyes and nodded as she faced him. "Yes, it was. Are you hungry, Grandpa? I can make you some breakfast before I head to class."

"I could eat. But come here for a moment, Granddaughter."

Walking over to her grandfather, she peered into his eyes and her heart was moved to see such concern lit in his eyes. "What's wrong? What happened?"

"Nothing you need to worry about."

"That boy make you cry?"

"Not exactly." Smiling, she shook her head as she sighed. "Life made me cry a long time ago, Grandpa. I'll start on breakfast."

Elise agreed to meet in the parking lot thirty minutes before school that day so they could talk about what happened. Natalie poured out her heart, unfiltered.

"When I saw him lying on that couch with the booze right by his head, I thought immediately of Martin. I freaked."

"Oh, honey. I don't blame you one iota! And that story about his juice being drugged? Oh, come on! Who would honestly buy that? People don't just hand out drugs this day and age. They keep them close!"

Even now, Natalie found herself defending him for some strange reason. "He doesn't lie, so it seems strange that he would now."

"Well, he probably didn't have to lie up until this point!" Shaking her head, Elise looked over at her as they sat together in the car. "You cut ties now, girl. Take this as a sign from God or whatever. Now you can focus on your grandpa and school and you don't have to waste a bunch of years with him trying to figure out that he isn't a good guy."

"That's true. Maybe it's a gift."

"You're going to be okay, Natalie. I promise."

Arriving home after school that afternoon around four o'clock, she found her grandfather in bed watching westerns.

"Did you move around today, Grandpa?"

"Not much. I've been feeling extremely tired today."

"Okay. I'll go start on dinner."

He sighed deeply, stopping her steps out from the bedroom. She turned toward him.

"It's fish tonight. Isn't it?"

Natalie nodded, her chin dipping. Remembering a request from her grandfather shortly after she had moved out to the farm, she broke into a smile and lifted her head. "How about we go grab some cheeseburgers and fries?"

He smiled. "Let's go before you change your mind!"

Helping him out to the car, she buckled him into the seat

and then came around to the driver's side and got in. She turned the key over.

"Hey."

Natalie looked over at him with a raised eyebrow. "Yeah, Grandpa?"

"Why are you doing this?"

"I think a better question is why not?" Smiling, she pulled out of the driveway and the two of them headed to Zips.

Arriving at their booth, Natalie set the tray of food down between them. Clay leaned over the fries and burgers and inhaled. "Oh, how I have missed that wonderful smell!"

After praying, they dug in. Clay began to tell stories from what it was like raising her father, Gerald, as a young boy and one instance of when Clay and Rose had taken him and his sister, Gabby, to a fast food joint on the north side of Spokane when he was eight. He had met another boy who was younger than him at the play place, and when Gerald had learned that the boy didn't get a kid's meal, he gave the boy his own toy.

"That was the first time I saw Gerald becoming a man. He was putting another person before himself. Did you know that's why he's so successful in his career?"

"Really?"

"Oh, yeah." Clay wiped his mouth with a napkin as he began to recap all of her dad's achievements from throughout his career. "When he sold that house for over two million—you remember, the one right out on the lake."

"Long Lake? In Suncrest?"

"Yes! That one! He had sold it to that guy because of how your father treated him. He is that way with all of his clients. It doesn't matter if it's a $110,000 house or a $2,000,000 mansion. He makes people feel valued, important, and irreplaceable. I know that hasn't transferred well over into family life since your mom passed. Personally, he and I have never been close. I've always hoped that one day, that would change, but who knows? I pray he at least one day comes back to a close relationship with you."

"Wow. I had no idea about that with my dad—the selling part. I knew about the change since Mom passed . . ."

Setting his cheeseburger down, Clay peered into Natalie's eyes. "Losing someone is difficult. When you lose a person, you lose a part of your heart and it leaves a hole ten miles wide and twenty miles deep. It's the hardest trial to go through."

"That's what I've been told, and that's what I've been learning from those letters between you and Grandma."

"You still reading those?"

"Yeah, I was . . ."

"But . . ."

Natalie smiled and shook her head. "Nothing, Grandpa."

"If you're meant to be with Jake, it'll happen. It'll all work out. Don't worry."

"Thanks, Grandpa."

That evening, after she helped her grandpa to bed, Natalie went to her bedroom and opened up the box of letters. Lifting another from the pile inside, she opened it up and began to read. The letters had replaced her novel reading entirely since she had found them in the attic. She found it much more interesting to dive into the real life and relationship between her grandparents.

Clay,

Even though you're away on business right now, I find it incredibly hard to be happy with you at the moment. Little Gerald won't stop reminding me of how you're not around and I can't stand it. Today, while I was out tending the lavender plants on the side of the house, I saw a butterfly and it made me think about the old days and the farm you were working on in Montana when we were kids a decade ago. Wow. Time sure has flown by over these years, and yet my love for you has not run dry or diminished in any capacity. Honestly, it's quite the opposite! My love grows deeper with each passing day. FYI - I get to die first, because I can't fathom a life without you, nor would I want to.

Love,
Rose

WIPING a tear as Natalie thought about how her grandmother wanted it the way it happened, her before him, she shook her head and peered up at the ceiling. "God, I don't know if Jacob is a good man of God or the one You have in mind for me, but I pray that You reveal to me what Your will is in the coming days, weeks, and months. Your goodness will remain no matter what happens. I know that. Amen."

Setting the letter down on the nightstand beside the lamp, she grabbed her Bible and picked up where she left off in the morning before she arose from bed. Philippians, chapter two. She read verse after verse, pausing and praying where she felt led to do so. Then, she came into chapter four.

Rejoice in the Lord always. I will say it again: Rejoice!
Let your gentleness be evident to all. The Lord is near.
Do not be anxious about anything, but in every situation, by prayer and petition, with thanksgiving, present your requests to God.
And the peace of God, which transcends all understanding, will guard your hearts and your minds in Christ Jesus.
Philippians 4:4-7

Pausing, she prayed. "God, let my heart rejoice *always*. Not some of the time. Not only when things are going the way I think they should, but *always*. You, Lord, know what I need more than I do. I merely want. Help me to rely on Your truths, Lord. Hold my heart up in Your arms, Lord. And help me to not worry or be anxious about anything in my life. Instead, let Your strength come to me. Fill me with Your peace, Your goodness, and Your Spirit, Lord. Help me let You reign over, in, and through my heart for all of my days. Amen."

Continuing, she read verse eight and the depths of her heart stirred with a comfort that was nothing short of divine and supernatural.

Finally, brothers and sisters, whatever is true, whatever is noble,
whatever is right, whatever is pure, whatever is lovely,
whatever is admirable—if anything is excellent or praiseworthy—
think about such things.
Philippians 4:8

This verse was what her heart needed in this very moment. This passage in the Word of God wasn't just typography on a page but the very breath of God's truth breathing into her heart and soul. She could feel the chains loosening and freedom rushing in. She hadn't any need to worry or dwell on her grandfather and his dying. She hadn't any need to worry or dwell on the fact that the greatest man she had ever met was now out of her life. This little morsel of wisdom was the direction she needed and so desperately craved in her soul.

Tears began to stream down her cheeks as thankfulness filled her. Lifting her eyes up to the ceiling, she closed them tightly and lifted her hands upward. "Let my thinking honor You every moment of the day. Let my soul worship You alone with my thoughts and actions. Help me to trust in You alone! You have pulled me out of the wreckage of my own self-destruction and saved me from disaster. Let me never stray from You again, God. Amen."

CHAPTER 12

*S*inking himself into work, Jacob was able to dull the heartache that followed the conversation with Natalie. He understood that she needed to focus on her grandfather, but he wasn't ignorant to the fact that she hadn't believed his story about Mercedes drugging him. The eight weeks that followed were painfully long and often ended with Jacob crawling into bed out of sheer exhaustion. He knew if he went to bed any sooner, he'd lie awake thinking of only her. Just six months ago, there wasn't a woman on the planet who could distract his thoughts away from God. Now she was just a field away from him, but farther than ever.

One morning, after running on the treadmill, he started in on a circuit of weight lifting when he heard his doorbell ring.

Dropping the dumbbells on the mat, he grabbed his towel from the bench and wiped his face as he exited his weight room to go answer it. A part of him hoped for the impossible, that it was Natalie.

Opening the door, he saw a very broken Andrew. Contrite in spirit and appearing to be wrecked emotionally,

Andrew's face wore a frown like it had been permanently etched into him.

Unable to control the power of the Spirit of God inside of him, Jacob was moved with compassion for his old friend. Ignoring that compassion, he glared. "What are you doing here, Andrew?"

"I didn't know where else to go . . ." His words trailed off, falling to the wayside out on the porch.

This man had contributed to Jacob's losing Natalie, and yet, he still looked upon him with love. God's love reached beyond the human boundaries of understanding inside Jacob. Peering at the person he'd once considered a friend, Jacob was able to see Andrew was ready for surrender. Pushing open the screen door, Jacob stepped aside. "Come on in, brother."

As Andrew's cheeks moistened with tears and his shoulders slumped with humility, Jacob was again moved in his heart. He immediately thought of how the Lord loves the humble. Jacob knew all of what was happening inside of him was a work of the Holy Spirit because he didn't have a generous bone in his body toward Andrew.

"Go ahead and grab a seat. I need to splash some water on my face, and I'll grab us some coffee."

Walking down the hallway, Jacob could feel a war raging inside him. One side, his flesh, was screaming at the top of its lungs. *Everything wrong with you and Natalie is that guy's fault! How could you let him back into your home after what he did? After what Mercedes did!* The other side simply said, *love my people.* The other side also reminded him of Jesus's interaction at the well with the prostitute and the many other encounters in which Jesus chose love over punishment.

Praying in the bathroom as he scooped handfuls of cold water into his face, he asked the Lord for wisdom and strength. "This is all You, Lord. I have no part. Lead me and my words."

As he finished washing up and toweled his face, he looked into the mirror. *God likes it when we fully know we have nothing to do with what's going on.* Chills ran the length of his spine and he shut off the light in the bathroom and returned down the hallway.

Entering the living room a few minutes later with two fresh cups of coffee from the kitchen, he handed one to Andrew and sat down beside him on the couch.

"I can't believe you let me in. I thought it was stupid when I had the idea to come over here. I told myself on the way over that you'd never open that door for me."

"I wouldn't open that door." Smiling, Jacob took a drink of his coffee and then set it down on the coffee table. "But Jesus would, and that's why I let you inside, brother. You've obviously been spat out by the world."

Andrew sighed deeply and nodded. He took a drink of his coffee. "God can't forgive me for what I've done to Marie, what I've done to you, and most of all, what I've done while calling myself a Christian!" Tears streamed down his cheeks as hopelessness rested in his eyes. "I've taken what was good in my life and trashed it."

Resting a hand on Andrew's back, Jacob nodded. "You've sinned, brother, but there is hope for you."

Turning to Jacob, he tilted his head. "You think so?"

"I know so." His own past flashed through his mind for a moment. "All you have to do is surrender, Andrew. Give it all over to God. He loves you so much that He became flesh and dwelt among us, and then He sacrificed Himself for you and for me. If you were the only one on earth, He still would've died. He doesn't want you to follow a bunch of rules or checklists, brother. He wants your heart. He wants a relationship with you. That's what knowing Jesus Christ is truly about. Yes, He saved us from Hell, but He also created a way for us to be in fellowship with Him."

"But after what I've done?"

"*Brother* . . . If you so much as look at a woman, you have committed adultery in your heart. If you have hated someone, you've murdered. We're imperfect, flawed people, and it's only Jesus's righteousness that can make us whole. It's only Him who can remove our sin. You are cleansed through the blood of Jesus Christ alone and not because of any works you can do."

He started to cry, pinching the bridge of his nose as he hunched over. "I don't deserve that kind of love!"

"You're right. You don't. But neither do I nor anyone else. I've been trying to help you see the reality of God's love for a while now, Andrew. Loving your wife like Christ loves the church isn't about loving her when she's perfect. It's not about loving the perfect person for you. It's loving your wife despite how imperfect she is. *That* is God's love to us."

Nodding, Andrew appeared to relax as he sat upright. "This day forward, I am recommitting myself to the Lord. I can't go on living the way I have been living."

"Amen, brother."

Gwen flew out to Spokane when she heard Clay had only a day or two left to live. Gathered around in the living room at the farmhouse, all of Clay's loved ones were there by his side as the nurses kept him as comfortable as possible. Tears were abounding in numbers, and Natalie hadn't seen her father so upset as she did this day. Exiting the living room to go grab something to eat in the kitchen, she lifted an apple from a bowl of fruit.

"You seem relatively calm today." Gwen dabbed her eyes with a tissue as she entered the kitchen.

Natalie turned and peered out at the oak tree in the front yard. Smiling, she shrugged a shoulder. "I've been with him for months, Sis. I've known this day was coming. Soon, he'll be with Jesus and Grandma."

Biting into the apple, she looked at her sister as she sat down in a chair at the table. Gwen's gaze shifted to the floor. "Maybe I should've come and been here too."

Walking over to her sister, Natalie placed a hand on her shoulder. "It's okay that you weren't. You have a life and family back in Wisconsin."

"Yeah, I guess."

Chrissy walked in. "Hey, you two. He's about to pass."

Gwen rose, and Natalie went with her sister into the living room. As soon as he passed, it was if Natalie could sense her grandfather's spirit was no longer there. An eerie feeling set across her entire being in that very moment. Spotting her father crying only a few feet away, she went over and wrapped her arms around her dad.

"It's okay, Dad. We'll see him again."

Natalie realized that all those worries and fears that her father had been building up inside himself about her weren't about her at all. They were about him. He was the one who was struggling the hardest. He was the one who was feeling the far more brutal side of the passing. While Natalie was sad to see her grandfather leave Earth, she knew he was much happier now on the other side of eternity.

A few days later, after the funeral, Natalie rode in the backseat of the car on the way back to the farmhouse with her father and Chrissy in the front seat. Natalie stared out the window from her seat. Memories of the prior months filed through her mind. The burger they finally had, the talks over meals, and the conversations about her grandmother,

Rose. Natalie smiled. She spent the hours following his passing reading more of the letters between him and Grandma. Though he was gone now, it was as if a small part of him still lived on through the written words he had penned.

"*Dad?*"

Her father glanced over his shoulder, then back to the road. "Yeah, Pumpkin?"

"Did you ever read those letters your mom and dad wrote to each other before they married and left Plains, Montana?"

Furrowing his eyebrows, he glanced back at her once more. "No. We weren't allowed. Why?"

Smiling as she peered out her window again, she felt her grandpa's love radiate through her heart. He had shared a part of his life he hadn't shared with others. Pulling out the last letter he wrote Grandma, and the letter she had carried with her since he passed away, she read it again.

ROSE,

I know you don't want to see me again, but I can't let this love go that I have for you. It's everything I ever wanted, and I can't take no for an answer. I'm meeting with Steve tonight to discuss a plan I have to get out. Here's to hope and here's to love's eternal flame that I feel still burns between you and me.

Love forever and always,

Clay

HER EYES MOISTENED and she slipped the aged note back into the envelope and returned it to her jacket pocket. Natalie's prayers and desires still rested in Jacob, but she couldn't pull herself to believe that he was the one for her. He hadn't visited, hadn't fought, hadn't done a thing to show that he was still interested in the slightest. She feared that going after him would be no different from her attempts to make it work with Martin for all those years. She couldn't do that.

Arriving at the farm, Natalie bowed her head and prayed for inner strength as she knew what was coming next. Saying goodbye to the memories she had stored up in her heart over the last five months. The walks up on the hill, the laughter underneath the oak tree, and the time spent learning and loving the man her grandfather was and had become. He was a special man, a far more special man than she had known even six months ago. Now he was gone, but she was better for the experience, even if losing him did hurt.

Leaving her father and Chrissy in the kitchen as they talked plans for all the "stuff" in the house, she went down the hallway to Clay's bedroom. She hadn't been inside since he passed. The door was shut. Leaning her head against the post outside the door, she closed her eyes and let herself pretend for a moment that he was on the other side, lying in bed. Her imagination even allowed her to hear *Gunsmoke* blaring on the television set. It hurt to think of him, but in a way, it also brought her comfort. Knocking lightly on the door, she pushed it open and walked in.

The bed was made perfectly, and there was no Grandpa Clay.

Letting herself fall across the bed, her heart began to twist inside her chest, and she wept hard. As the tears slowed, she quietly rolled over and stared up at the ceiling. Turning her head toward the glass bookcase in front of the windows, she saw a glass cube she didn't recognize. Rising to her feet, she went over to the shelf and lifted the cube for a closer look. Inside was a sparkling red rose and she smiled. *Grandpa . . .*

"Hey, Pumpkin?" Her father's voice startled her, and she whipped around to face him.

"You about ready? Your Aunt Gabby is going to take care

of everything here. She's on her way out. I can drop you off in town if you have everything packed and ready to go."

"I have my car, Dad. Thanks, though."

"Okay. I love you. Come here." His open arms brought a rushing wave of comfort to her hurting heart in the moment, and she rushed over to him. They embraced in a long hug in the moment. "Hey."

She peered up at her father.

"I'm going to try harder to be a better dad to you. I know I've put work as a priority for a long time now, and that's going to change. I promise."

Smiling, she hugged him tighter. *He does care . . .*

"I want you to come over for Thanksgiving dinner tomorrow night. If you can."

"I'd love to, Dad."

A smile rested on his lips and they released from the embrace. "Good. See you then."

Turning back to the shelf, she walked over and set the rose cube down. Taking one more look at the rose in the glass, she smiled. "I'll never forget you two." Then she left the room.

Packing her car with all of her belongings, Natalie shut the trunk and caught Smokey out in the barn. After getting her cat into the carrier in the passenger seat, she went to get into the driver side of the car. Just as she got in and turned the key over, she saw Jacob walking through the field. Her heart jumped. She hesitated to put the car into gear and leave. After the day she'd had, she wanted to speak with him more than ever. *I should say goodbye, at least.* Shutting off the car, she got out and walked over to the fence line to meet him.

"Hey." He glanced at her black dress for a moment before turning his eyes back to hers.

"Yeah."

"That's too bad. How are you holding up?"

"It hurts."

"I bet."

"I'm going back to Spokane today."

Worry lit in his eyes. "Where's that leave us?"

Her heart and her head didn't match. While she'd love to climb into his arms and let his lips serenade her in his affections and melt away all the pain inside her heart, she feared that he'd hurt her. The story he gave still didn't make sense to her, and if he had lied . . . she'd be investing in a future with someone she couldn't trust. Glancing back at her car as she tried to buy a moment to respond, she simply shrugged. "I don't know, Jake. I loved spending time with you, and I loved what we had, but I think it's over."

"It's not over for me. I refuse."

Her heart melted at his words. "But why? Maybe it should be over."

"Because I can't go a day without thinking of you. I wake up, you're there. I work, you're there. I go to sleep, you're there." Pressing a hand against his chest, he shook his head. "I've been trying to forget you, but my heart won't let me."

"The heart can be deceitful, Jake. I'm sorry."

Turning around, she walked away. Doing so was the hardest thing she had ever done, but she knew she couldn't let the desires of her heart trump the reality that was present. The reality was that she didn't know Jacob as well as she thought she did. Wiping tears as she walked to the car, she prayed for strength in moving forward.

CHAPTER 13

*P*icking up shifts at a restaurant in Spokane, Natalie was able to fill part of her free time by working. Her other free time was spent down at Pines Baptist Church, volunteering in various ministries. Working at an upper-class restaurant on the north side of Spokane, Natalie made decent tips nightly and was able to keep herself engaged socially by meeting new people all the time, both at work and at church. Four months had already gone by since she left the farm in November, but she still thought of her time there with a deep fondness.

The apartment that once felt like a prison was now her carved out place in the world where God was at the center, and love flowed freely through it. The romance novels that once lined the bookshelf now held Bible studies, inspirational stories, and a picture of her father and herself.

Natalie's time with her grandfather was a treasure she would never forget and an influence on her life that would never end. Her time with Jacob felt like the healing and love that her soul had desperately needed after Martin in order to be set on the path of God's will in her life. She hoped Jacob was doing well but hadn't had contact with him since the cold goodbye on the day of Clay's funeral.

On her way out of school to the parking lot, Elise caught up to her side. "You want to hang tonight?"

"Can't. I have work."

"Oh, yeah. That's right. You are choosing to work."

"Hey, now. Be nice, Elise."

"Psh. I know. I just don't get why you can't handle handouts from your rich dad. We had our third kid just for the tax benefit! Kidding, kidding."

Smiling, Natalie ran through her schedule in her mind. "I'm free tomorrow, if you want to do something."

"Yeah. Tonight was it. I have kids, and the babysitter was saying she was free tonight."

"Where's Tony?"

"Atlanta, on business."

"I'm sorry!"

"It's all good. Next time." Elise put her sunglasses on, and they parted ways.

Getting into her car, Natalie paused and pulled her cell phone out. She hadn't enough time that morning to pray over everyone and everything she wanted to, and she was feeling imbalanced all day because of it. Breathing in deeply, then expelling the air from her lungs, she opened the app on her phone and began to pray. As she prayed earnestly to the Lord, she attached Scriptures and truths from the Word of God to what she was praying. The power she gained through prayer had intensified in the last six months as she was growing closer in her walk with the Lord.

"Our Father, who is in heaven, hallowed be your name, your kingdom come; your will be done, on earth as it is in heaven. Let Your will be done in my life, Jesus. Let it accomplish the purposes You propose, not what I propose.

Give us this day our daily bread. Let me not easily forget

what Your Word is and what Your truth is, Lord. You lead me, instruct me, and show me the way to everlasting joy through Your precious Word. On those days I don't feel like reading the Bible, let me push in more. For Your word feeds my soul, and Your Word will never pass away or leave me.

And forgive us our trespasses, as we forgive those who trespass against us. *Oh, Lord!* My soul cries out as You reveal more and more in me that I need forgiveness for. Right when I think I'm doing okay, You open my eyes to see more. The forgiveness You give goes on and on. Help me to forgive others like You have been so gracious to forgive me.

Lead us not into temptation, but deliver us from evil. I need Your help, Lord. Every single day and in every single way. Help me to avoid temptation. Let temptation not even fall on my doorstep, but if it does, I pray for the strength to turn away from it, escape it. And every form of evil, Lord, I am asking You to deliver me from it.

For Yours is the kingdom, the power, and the glory, forever and ever. Amen. Your kingdom will never pass away, God. Help me to remember that when I'm confronted with this worldly kingdom that *is* passing away. God, You have *all* of the power. You alone deserve all of the glory. I pray that you help me live my life in a way that brings You glory and praise and worship every single day."

She continued to pray for the people on the list. Her friend Elise, teachers, co-workers, and even Jacob was on that list. While she hadn't seen him in quite some time, she still prayed for him every day. He was a pleasant memory and the man who had taught her the importance of deepening the connection and relationship between herself and God.

After praying in her car in the college parking lot, she backed out of the parking stall and drove to work.

Clocking in on the computer at the serving station she

was working at, she tied her apron around her waist and went to go wait on tables. When she first started waiting tables, she was terrible at it, but her trainer was patient and taught her everything she needed to know in her first month and a half. Almost quitting a few times, it was a stressful job for Natalie, but it paid well and helped her not be so dependent on her father's money. It was hard enough to know he was still paying for her college. This was her way of providing at least something.

JACOB'S CELL phone rang with an unknown number. Not sure if it was an interested buyer or just another scammer calling, he answered reluctantly.

"This is Jake."

"Hi, this is Google with an important message regarding your business—"

Click.

It had already been two months of having his cabin on the market, and he couldn't seem to find a buyer as of March. He had a few offers, but they were too low. He wanted out of Chattaroy and wanted to move back to the Big Apple. It had to do partly with the tormenting thoughts of his time with Natalie, but he had himself convinced it was more than just that. Jacob missed the city and the hustle that filled the atmosphere working at the New York Stock Exchange. Old friends and colleagues were eager to get him back, several offering him a place to stay until he got on his feet. All he had to do was sell the cabin and he could get out.

Walking over to the window facing the field and the farm, he peered out at the acreage. A construction site sat atop where the barn used to stand. The new owners had plans to tear down the farmhouse once they were finished with rebuilding the barn. The day they tore the barn down, Jacob was over there, screaming at them to stop, but he was forced off the property. His heart broke for Clay, and for Natalie too. He almost called her once to speak with her about how upset he was to see the barn and all their hard work on the roof come tumbling down, but he refused himself. He didn't want to bother her.

Staring at Clay's old property, he prayed. "A good barn, a good house, and fine people were there, Lord. Why'd that have to change?"

His cell phone rang again. He looked at the screen. Another local number, but just as easily a scam. He tapped to answer.

"This is Jake."

"Hello. You the one with a cabin for sale out in Chattaroy?"

Walking over to the couch, he sat as a smile grew on his lips. "Why, yes, I am."

The man came out within the hour to look over the property and get a tour of the cabin. The man was middle-aged, in his late forties. "Why'd you build it, if you don't mind me asking?"

Peering around, Jacob opened his palms. "Take a look around. The view is impeccable!"

The man pointed at the farm. "Except for the construction site next door."

"Right, a temporary inconvenience. You want to take a look inside?"

"Sure."

Leading the man inside, he gave a tour of his cabin. As he pointed out the custom built-ins, the unique weight-room design, and the sauna, Jacob started to backtrack in his mind over selling it. As they ended in the kitchen, Jacob looked at the man who was interested in the cabin.

"If you don't mind my asking, what do you plan to do with the cabin, sir? A getaway? A home?"

"I plan to rip it down and build four houses on the plot of land."

Jacob shook his head in bewilderment. "Why would you do that?"

"Because I can make more money that way. Why does it matter to you?"

Resting a hand on his wood crafted support beam he hewed by hand, he sighed deeply. "This place means a lot to me. It's not for sale anymore. Sorry for wasting your time."

CHAPTER 14

*O*ne Saturday afternoon, three months later in June, while Natalie was waiting on a table outside on the patio at the restaurant, she recognized a woman. Natalie couldn't place her face, but she knew that she had seen her before. Toward the end of the woman's meal with a man, she took off her sunglasses and stared at her.

Shaking a finger, the woman nodded. "I know you. You were that random woman who came over looking for the prude last summer."

Natalie, with hands full of empty plates, stopped and looked at her. "What?"

"Out in the country. I was with one of my ex-boyfriends at the time." The woman hushed her date as he looked uncomfortable. "Don't you worry. He's out of the picture." Turning back to Natalie, she continued. "I don't remember his name, either of them, frankly. Ha! But I know the cabin's owner was a total prude, and you came looking for him the one night I was partying there."

"*Oh.* You must be one of Andrew's friends."

"Yes! I remember that guy now. The idiot went back to

his wife." The man got up from the table and left his date there with Natalie. The woman shook her head and laughed but followed suit, rising from her seat. She paused her steps at Natalie and lowered her voice. "If you see that prudish religious man, tell him I hope he had a nice sleep. Ha!"

As she winked, she laughed and walked away.

Natalie dropped the plates in her hand, sending them scattering across the floor, breaking. *He wasn't lying . . .*

When her shift ended, she got in her car and drove out to Chattaroy. Her pulse raced and her hopes were higher than the clouds above. Natalie only hoped it wasn't too late. She prayed that Jacob was still waiting for her.

Pulling into the driveway, she parked in front of his cabin. Seeing a pretty woman through the window inside the living room, her heart sank.

Hope drained out of her as she lowered her head to the steering wheel. She began to cry and pray. "God, why?"

Knock, knock

Lifting her head from the steering wheel, she looked over through her driver's side window to see Jacob standing on the other side. Her heart began to beat again, and she pushed open the door as he backed out of the way.

"What's going on? I thought you . . ." She glanced at the cabin.

"That's a friend from the homeless shelter. She was dropping off the schedule for this month at the soup kitchen."

Standing there with Jacob was surreal. Turning her head, she looked out at the field nearby. It felt like so long ago, but at the same time, so recent. She could feel her heart stirring as she strolled across the tall grass over to his cabin like it had just happened.

"I bought it."

Coming to, she shook her head in confusion. Natalie's eyes came back to Jacob's gaze. "What?"

He pointed to the farm in the distance. "The farm. I bought it."

Sticking out her head, her eyes widened. "I thought they were tearing it all down."

Her gaze fell on the farm as he continued speaking.

"That was the original plan of the owners who bought it, but they only got the barn pulled down before I realized I wanted it in the Spring. I was able to keep the farmhouse intact. That's the good news."

Her heart began to pound hard as she realized he had done it for her. Eyes moistening, Natalie shook her head. "I should've believed you, Jake."

"What do you mean?"

"Your story . . . about Mercedes. The truth is that I didn't believe you. I had been hurt so badly before by Martin that I couldn't risk being with you."

"I understand if you still can't believe me." His chin dipped and he shook his head. "I shouldn't have been in the position I was in that night. It was my fault."

Natalie took a step closer to him and placed her hands on each side of his face, lifting his eyes to hers. "I saw Mercedes today. I know you were telling the truth, and I'm so sorry I never believed you."

AFTER DINNER THAT EVENING, Jacob walked with Natalie over to the farmhouse. As they walked the field, he turned toward her.

"We never really talked much about our first marriages. Did you want to talk about them?"

She shrugged and glanced over at him for a moment, then looked forward. "I don't know, Jake. It's in the past and for now, I don't see any point in doing so."

"I just worry that you'll take off again. If you had this kind of painful past . . ."

She stopped and turned toward him. Grabbing both of his hands, she peered into his eyes and right into his soul.

"I'm sorry for that, but I can assure you it'll never happen again. I don't think I was fully healed until I went back to Spokane and spent some time on my own. God showed me life can be beautiful and that I am loved, fully and wholly, by Him."

That reassuring statement brought an unmeasurable level of comfort to Jacob and his plan once they reached the farm. Smiling, he said, "Good."

They continued walking.

Arriving at the farm and the white fence, she stopped and stuck her head out as she looked out into the field toward the hill. "Is that a cow out there?"

"Yeah. A familiar, friendly face."

"No way! It's Betsy?"

Natalie took off in a sprint toward Betsy. Jacob couldn't stop smiling as he watched the woman he loved run across the field toward the silly old cow that had brought the two of them together.

As he came the final few steps to Betsy and Natalie, he saw that she had found the secured neck collar that had hung around Betsy's neck for the last three months. On the collar was a small worn box about the size of a quarter on each side. It had a small button that was fastened to a flap. She pulled it open and out popped the beautiful diamond ring he had bought the day he refused to sell his cabin. Heart pounding, he dropped to one knee as she turned to him with the ring in her hand.

"How . . . ?"

"I bought it the day I knew I'd wait forever for you."

"But how did you know I'd come back?"

"I didn't know if you ever would. But I had *hope*. I told myself and I told God that if you ever come back, I'd ask your hand in marriage. So, Natalie Townsend. Will you marry me?"

"Yes!"

CHAPTER 15

*J*n August of that same year, they married beneath the old oak tree. Everyone she loved and cared about was in attendance, and those who had passed on before were there in spirit. After the ceremony was over, and the after celebration was well underway into the evening, her daddy asked her to dance.

Her heart full and her eyes wet with tears, she placed her hand in her father's and joined him out on the wood dance floor beneath the starry night sky. She and her father had grown close following the passing of her grandfather. She contributed it to a combination of losing his father and realizing that his family still needed him even if they were all grown.

"Walking Gwen down the aisle was easy, but walking you down the aisle has never been quite the same as with her."

Lifting her face from her father's shoulder, Natalie looked at him with a smile. "Why is that, Dad?"

"You're my little Pumpkin."

She couldn't stop smiling, and they continued to dance. After the sweet moment with her father on the dance floor, she returned to her groom who had found his way over to his friend Andrew's table.

"Hi, Andrew. Hi, Marie."

The both of them smiled and said hello back. Andrew and Marie had found their way back to love and each other through the power of prayer and turning their hearts to God. It was a beautiful testimonial of God's ability to help those who turn to Him.

"Yo, Jake. You want me to go grab it? They said it was ready."

Confusion entered Natalie's mind as she turned toward Jacob. "What's he talking about?"

Jacob laughed. "Yeah, man. Go."

Turning toward his bride as Andrew got up and left the celebration, he brought his hands up to her arms and dipped his eyes as he stared into her gaze. "*Listen* . . . I got something for you."

"What? Why?" She laughed. "We aren't supposed to get each other something on our wedding day!"

"I know, but I did."

"Tell me what it is."

Jacob tightened his lips as he backed away with a grin. "Nope. Not happening."

Elise came over to her, distracting her away from the surprise.

"How do you do it?"

Natalie shook her head. "What do you mean?"

"You've been in that dress for hours and still look *amazing*."

Natalie laughed.

"Oh, whatever. Where's your hubby?"

"I think he's at the drinks table, getting some more punch."

"Sorry there isn't a whole lot of food. I know we ran out pretty early."

Playfully smacking her, Elise shook her head. "Are you kidding me? It's been the best wedding we've ever been to! Plus, just getting a break from the kids is a pleasant break in life. Speaking of kids . . . you two going to jump right into family making?"

Smiling as she thought about children, she shrugged. "I don't know. I'm pretty sure we won't waste time. He wants to have like five kids."

"Whoa. Five?" Shaking her head, Elise came in closer. "Don't have five kids. I have three and I want to seriously freak out some days. It's hard."

Laughing, Natalie shook her head. "You're a great encouragement!"

"I'm sorry. Have lots of kids!" Elise's gaze fell on Jacob and she smiled. Looking back at Natalie, she said, "I was wrong about him. He isn't like other men."

"God has that effect on the human heart."

"I'm starting to see that truth the more I get to know you, Natalie. I treasure our friendship and I'm really glad we met."

"Me too."

Hearing the sound of a puppy a little while later brought confusion into Natalie's mind. Searching the crowd still gathered at tables and on the dance floor, she tried to pinpoint the location of the dog.

Then, she caught Jacob's face as he approached through the crowd. Finding his smile in her view, her heart warmed as he came closer. A final person stepped out of the way, and a little German Shepherd puppy came into view in Jacob's arms.

"What is this cute little guy doing here?" Smiling, Natalie patted the puppy's head, then rubbed lightly behind his ear.

"My gift."

"Oh?"

"Natalie, meet Bruce." Jacob smiled.

"What? That's weird." She kept petting the dog. "My grandpa had to shoot a dog named Bruce years ago. He always wanted to get another one."

"I know. You told me about Bruce and the letter that first summer we spent together."

Her heart melted as she stopped and looked up at him.

"You remembered?"

"I did." Jacob's eyes spoke of his love in that very moment.

Tears of love ran down her cheeks, and she stepped toward him, kissing him as she smiled.

ONE MONTH AFTER THEIR WEDDING, Jacob took it upon himself to surprise his wife again. She had loved the puppy so much, and the surprise of him purchasing the farmhouse and the cow, Betsy, back that he almost felt a compulsion to keep surprising her. This time, it would be epic, and he knew that she would love it.

When her car pulled into the driveway and over the bridge, he promptly logged off his stock market monitoring software and exited the farmhouse to go greet her. His heart pounding and his excitement crackling inside, he lifted a prayer to Heaven above.

"Thank You, God. My life is so perfect, so sublime! You've blessed me with an amazing woman of God, and now this. This is going to be great. Your goodness, Your plans, Your everything are so much better than I ever expected or could expect. Help me not to forget it. Amen."

STEPPING OUT OF HER CAR, she shut the door and looked eagerly forward to getting inside and seeing her husband. Though they had only been married for a month, she felt like she had already known him for a lifetime.

As she walked between the trees, she saw Jacob standing out on the sidewalk. Her heart fluttered at seeing him and she approached with a smile on her lips.

"What's going on?"

He laughed and took her by the hand. "Can't a husband just come out and greet his lovely, lovely wife?"

She shrugged, still smiling. "I suppose . . ."

They walked together and made it inside. As he shut the door behind her, she loosened her backpack and purse and set them down on the couch.

"C'mon, sugar." He again took her by the hand. She laughed at seeing how excited he was to show her something. He led her through the hallway and to the spare room. "Close your eyes."

Closing her eyes, she could hear him turn the doorknob and open the door. She wondered, *What? Did you clean the spare room and all the clutter?*

She heard the light switch turn on.

Suddenly, Jacob's hands were on her arms and he moved her into the room.

"Open 'em."

Natalie opened her eyes, and as she did, they grew wider as she looked around the room. It was a baby nursery. He had painted the whole room yellow and put up Noah's Ark animals on the walls. A white crib sat in the corner and a dresser and changing station along with it.

Natalie's heart melted as she was overwhelmed by her husband's attention to her desires. She began to cry, covering her mouth as shock overtook every fiber of her being.

"Jacob . . ."

"You like it?"

She turned toward him. "I love it!"

Grabbing hold of him, she clung to him tightly. Jacob lifted her up and twirled her in a half-circle and then kissed her deeply. In that moment, Natalie felt the love not only of Jacob, but the love of God flowing in and through her heart. She had finally realized what it meant to be fully loved. Though she had lost a lot in her lifetime, what she'd gained by knowing Jacob and knowing Clay, and ultimately, knowing God's heart, had forever changed her life.

The End.

BOOK PREVIEWS

A REASON TO LIVE PREVIEW

Chapter 1

POUNDING COMING FROM THE FRONT door of his house on the South Hill woke Jonathan Dunken from sleep at three o'clock in the morning. Then the doorbell chimed, pulling him further away from his slumber and fully awake. He had only been asleep for an hour, as he had been up late the night before sketching building concepts for a client. He was the co-founder and sole architect of his and his brother Tyler's company, *Willow Design*. A company the two of them started just a few years ago, after Marie passed and Jonathan needed more work to throw himself into.

Pushing his eyelids open, he sat up in his bed, smoothing a hand over his face. *Who on earth is that?* He wondered. The doorbell chimed again, and he begrudgingly emerged from his bed and left his bedroom.

He traveled out from his room, through the long hallway, and down the glass stairs. As he entered the foyer, more pounding on the door sounded, edging his already growing irritation. He was ready to rip into whoever was on the other side of that door. But when he finally opened it, his heart plunged and the wind fanning his anger fell quiet. It was his sister-in-law, Shawna Gillshock, a woman he hadn't seen since the funeral four years ago.

Shawna looked just like he remembered her—a mess, her brunette hair disheveled, eyeliner mingled with rainwater ran down each of her cheeks. She was wearing a stained pair of ragged sweats three times too big and a ragged oversized hooded sweatshirt. He immediately noticed the sight of fresh blood on a cut near her left eyebrow.

"I need your help, Jonathan. I didn't know where else to go." Her voice was strained, filled with desperation. She jerked her head toward the car in the driveway. Sheets of rain and wind whipped back and forth in the night's air, dancing across the headlights of the car. "My dad wouldn't let me come to his house. I need a place for me and my daughter, Rose, to stay tonight. My boyfriend beat me again, and I'm leaving him for good this time. You're the only person I know that he doesn't know. Please?"

Jonathan was moved with compassion, though a part of him wanted to say 'no' to her. Deep down, somewhere beneath the pain and grief that followed losing his wife, he heard a whisper and felt a nudge. *Let her stay.*

"Okay. You can stay." He helped her inside with her luggage and daughter. The luggage she had brought didn't consist of much. A backpack and one suitcase. Once the two of them had everything inside the house in the foyer, he led the way to the guest room on the main floor of the two-story house. The room was tucked away at the end of the hallway. Opening the door, he flipped on the light switch. Two lamps, one on each nightstand on either side of the bed, turned on. Each of the nightstands, along with the dresser and crown molding, was stark white. The walls were a warm brown, not dark, but not light either. On the far side of the bedroom, near the dresser, was another doorway leading into an en-suite bathroom.

"Thank you so much for this." Her words were filled with genuine gratitude as she set her backpack on the bed. She turned and glanced at the TV on top of the dresser.

"How long do you think you'll be here, Shawna?" Jonathan was gently reminding her it wasn't a long-term solution but more of a friendly gesture in a time of need.

"Just a few days. I'm going to call my dad again tomorrow and see if I can convince him to let us stay there with him and Betty until I can figure something out."

The mention of her parents jogged painful memories that Jonathan had tried to forget. His parents had died his senior year of high school, so he only really had Marie's parents in his life. "Okay, and if he doesn't budge?"

Shawna turned to face him. "I'll figure something out. Don't worry about me, just thanks again for tonight."

Her daughter became fussy a moment later, a whimper escaping. "What's wrong, Rose?"

She touched her tummy. "I'm hungry."

"How old is she?"

Smiling, Shawna turned to him. "She's two. Talking away already. Do you have anything she can eat?"

Scrambling through the fridge in his mind, he shrugged. "Does she like tuna?"

"Um, not really. Do you have hot dogs, macaroni, or something more kid-friendly like that?"

"No, but there are eggs in the fridge. Sorry. I wasn't really prepared for you." He tipped a smile, trying to loosen the awkwardness and embrace the disturbance of the entire situation.

She laughed lightly. "It's totally fine. Eggs work great. She loves scrambled eggs. Thank you again, Jonathan. It means the world that you took us in tonight."

"Don't mention it. Do you need help cooking, or can you manage it?"

"It's pretty basic. I think I got it handled. You look like you need some sleep, so go ahead."

"I do need sleep. Going back to bed now. 'Night."

Leaving Shawna and Rose in the guest room, he shut the door quietly and thought of his late wife, Marie, as he made his way back to his bedroom upstairs. Shawna was his only sister-in-law, and she had made frequent appearances in his and Marie's life, but that had been years ago. Even back in the day, Shawna was always in need. Her life reminded him of a slow-moving train wreck in progress. Though her life was a wreck, Marie was always ready and willing to love on her and care for her when she was in need of her big sister. That was Marie's nature with not only family, but anyone who was in need.

Did you enjoy this free sample? Find it on Amazon

ONE THURSDAY MORNING PREVIEW

Prologue

To love and be loved—it was all I ever wanted. Nobody could ever convince me John was a bad man. He made me feel loved when I did not know what love was. I was his and he was mine. It was perfect . . . or at least, I thought it was.

I cannot pinpoint why everything changed in our lives, but it did—and for the worst. My protector, my savior, and my whole world came crashing down like a heavy spring downpour. The first time he struck me, I remember thinking it was just an accident. He had been drinking earlier in the day with his friends and came stumbling home late that night. The lights were low throughout the house because I had already gone to bed. I remember hearing the car pull up outside in the driveway. Leaping to my feet, I came rushing downstairs and through the kitchen to greet him. He swung, which I thought at the time was because I startled him, and the back side of his hand caught my cheek.

I should have known it wasn't an accident.

The second time was no accident at all, and I knew it. After a heavy night of drinking the night his father died, he came to the study where I was reading. Like a hunter looking for his prey, he came up behind me to the couch. Grabbing the back of my head and digging his fingers into my hair, he kinked my neck over the couch and asked me why I hadn't been faithful to him. I had no idea what he was talking about, so out of sheer fear, I began to cry. John took that as a sign of guilt and backhanded me across the face. It was hard enough to leave a bruise the following day. I stayed with him anyway. I'd put a little extra makeup on around my eyes or anywhere else when marks were left. I didn't stay because I was stupid, but because I loved him. I kept telling myself that our love could get us through this. The night of his father's death, I blamed his outburst on the loss of his father. It was too much for him to handle, and he was just letting out steam. I swore to love him through the good times and the bad. This was just one of the bad times.

Each time he'd hit me, I'd come up with a reason or excuse for the behavior. There was always a reason, at least in my mind, as to why John hit me. Then one time, after a really bad injury, I sought help from my mother before she passed away. The closest thing to a saint on earth, she dealt with my father's abuse for decades before he died. She was a devout Christian, but a warped idea of love plagued my mother her entire life. She told me, 'What therefore God hath joined together, let not man put asunder.' That one piece of advice she gave me months before passing made me suffer through a marriage with John for another five trying years.

Each day with John as a husband was a day full of prayer. I would pray for him not to drink, and sometimes, he didn't —those were the days I felt God had listened to my pleas. On the days he came home drunk and swinging, I felt alone, like God had left me to die by my husband's hands. Fear was a cornerstone of our relationship, in my eyes, and I hated it. As the years piled onto one another, I began to deal with two entirely different people when it came to John. There was the John who would give me everything I need in life and bring flowers home on the days he was sober, and then there was John, the drunk, who would bring insults and injury instead of flowers.

I knew something needed to desperately change in my life, but I didn't have the courage. Then one day, it all changed when two little pink lines told me to run and never look back.

Chapter 1

Fingers glided against the skin of my arm as I lay on my side looking into John's big, gorgeous brown eyes. It was morning, so I knew he was sober, and for a moment, I thought maybe, just maybe I could tell him about the baby growing inside me. Flashes of a shared excitement between us blinked through my mind. He'd love having a baby around the house. *He really would.* Behind those eyes, I saw the man I fell in love with years ago down in Town Square in New York City. Those eyes were the same ones that brought me into a world of love and security I had never known before. Moments like that made it hard to hate him. Peering over at his hand that was tracing the side of my body, I saw the cut on his knuckles from where he had smashed the coffee table a few nights ago. My heart retracted the notion of telling him about the baby. I knew John would be dangerous for a child.

Chills shivered up my spine as his fingers traced from my arm to the curve of my back. *Could I be strong enough to live without him?* I wondered as the fears sank back down into me. Even if he was a bit mean, he had a way of charming me like no other man I had ever met in my life. He knew how to touch gently, look deeply and make love passionately. It was only when he drank that his demons came out.

"Want me to make you some breakfast?" I asked, slipping out of his touch and from the bed to my feet. His touches were enjoyable, but I wanted to get used to not having them. My mind often jumped back and forth between leaving, not leaving, and something vaguely in between. It was hard.

John smiled up at me from the bed with what made me feel like love in his eyes. I suddenly began to feel bad about the plan to leave, but I knew he couldn't be trusted with a child. *Keep it together.*

"Sure, babe. That'd be great." He brought his muscular arms from out of the covers and put them behind his head. My eyes traced his biceps and face. Wavy brown hair and a jawline that was defined made him breathtakingly gorgeous. Flashes of last night's passion bombarded my mind. He didn't drink, and that meant one thing—we made love. It started in the main living room just off the foyer. I was enjoying my evening cup of tea while the fireplace was lit when suddenly, John came home early. I was worried at first, but when he leaned over the couch and pulled back my blonde hair, he planted a tender kiss on my neck. I knew right in that moment that it was going to be a good night. Hoisting me up from the couch with those arms and pressing me against the wall near the fireplace, John's passion fell from his lips and onto the skin of my neck as I wrapped my arms around him.

The heat between John and me was undeniable, and it

made the thoughts of leaving him that much harder. It was during those moments of pure passion that I could still see the bits of the John I once knew—the part of John that didn't scare me and had the ability to make me feel safe, and the part of him that I never wanted to lose.

"All right," I replied with a smile as I broke away from my thoughts. Leaving down the hallway, I pushed last night out of my mind and focused on the tasks ahead.

Retrieving the carton of eggs from the fridge in the kitchen, I shut the door and was startled when John was standing on the other side. Jumping, I let out a squeak. "John!"

He tilted his head and slipped closer to me. With nothing on but his boxer briefs, he backed me against the counter and let his hand slide the corner of my shirt up my side. He leaned closer to me. I felt the warmth of his breath on my skin as my back arched against the counter top. He licked his lips instinctively to moisten them and then gently let them find their way to my neck. "Serenah . . ." he said in a smooth, seductive voice.

"Let me make you breakfast," I said as I set the carton down on the counter behind me and turned my neck into him to stop the kissing.

His eyebrows rose as he pulled away from my body and released. His eyes met mine. There it was—the change. *"Fine."*

"What?" I replied as I turned and pulled down a frying pan that hung above the island counter.

"Nothing. Nothing. I have to go shower." He left down the hallway without a word, but I could sense tension in his tone.

Waiting for the shower to turn on after he walked into the bathroom and slammed the door, I began to cook his eggs. When a few minutes had passed and I hadn't heard the water start running, I lifted my eyes and looked down the hallway.

There he was.

John stood at the end of hallway, watching me. Standing in the shifting shadows of the long hallway, he was more than creepy. He often did that type of thing, but it came later in the marriage, not early on and only at home. I never knew how long he was standing there before I caught him, but he'd always break away after being seen. He had a sick obsession of studying me like I was some sort of weird science project of his.

I didn't like it all, but it was part of who he had become. *Not much longer,* I reminded myself.

I smiled down the hallway at him, and he returned to the bathroom to finally take his shower. As I heard the water come on, I finished the eggs and set the frying pan off the burner. Dumping the eggs onto a plate, I set the pan in the sink and headed to the piano in the main living room. Pulling the bench out from under the piano, I got down on my hands and knees and lifted the flap of carpet that was squared off. Removing the plank of wood that concealed my secret area, I retrieved the metal box and opened it.

Freedom.

Ever since he hit me that second time, a part of me knew we'd never have the forever marriage I pictured, so in case I was right, I began saving money here and there. I had been able to save just over ten thousand dollars. A fibbed high-priced manicure here, a few non-existent shopping trips with friends there. It added up, and John had not the foggiest clue, since he was too much of an egomaniac to pay attention to anything that didn't directly affect him. Sure, it was his money, but money wasn't really 'a thing' to us. We were beyond that. My eyes looked at the money in the stash and then over at the bus ticket to Seattle dated for four days from now. I could hardly believe it. I was really going to finally leave him after all this time. Amongst the cash and bus ticket, there was a cheap pay-as-you go cellphone and a fake ID. I had to check that box at least once a day ever since I found out about my pregnancy to make sure he hadn't found it. I was scared to leave, but whenever I felt that way, I rubbed my pregnant thirteen-week belly, and I knew I had to do what was best for *us*. Putting the box back into the floor, I was straightening out the carpet when suddenly, John's breathing settled into my ears behind me.

"What are you doing?" he asked, towel draped around his waist behind me. *I should have just waited until he left for work . . . What were you thinking, Serenah?* My thoughts scolded me.

Slamming my head into the bottom the piano, I grabbed my head and backed out as I let out a groan. "There was a crumb on the carpet."

"What? Underneath the piano?" he asked.

Anxiety rose within me like a storm at sea. Using the bench for leverage, I placed a hand on it and began to get up. When I didn't respond to his question quick enough, he shoved my arm that was propped on the piano bench, causing me to smash my eye into the corner of the bench. Pain radiated through my skull as I cupped my eye and began to cry.

"Oh, please. That barely hurt you."

I didn't respond. Falling the rest of the way to the floor, I cupped my eye and hoped he'd just leave. Letting out a heavy sigh, he got down, still in his towel, and put his hand on my shoulder. "I'm sorry, honey."

Jerking my shoulder away from him, I replied, "Go away!"

He stood up and left.

John hurt me sober? Rising to my feet, I headed into the half-bathroom across the living room and looked into the mirror. My eye was blood red—he had popped a blood vessel. Tears welled in my eyes as my eyebrows furrowed in disgust.

Four days wasn't soon enough to leave—I was leaving today.

Did you enjoy this free sample? Find it on Amazon

FREE GIFT

Cole has fought hundreds of fires in his lifetime, but he had never tasted fear until he came to fighting a fire in his own home. *Amongst The Flames* is a Christian firefighter fiction that tackles real-life situations and problems that exist in Christian marriages today. It brings with it passion, love and spiritual depth that will leave you feeling inspired. This Inspirational Christian romance novel is one book that you'll want to read over and over again.

To Claim Visit:
offer.tkchapin.com

One Saturday Evening (Book 3)

One Sunday Drive (Book 4)

One Monday Prayer (Book 5)

One Tuesday Lunch (Book 6)

One Wednesday Dinner (Book 7)

Embers & Ashes Series

Amongst the Flames (Book 1)

Out of the Ashes (Book 2)

Up in Smoke (Book 3)

After the Fire (Book 4)

Love's Enduring Promise Series

The Perfect Cast (Book 1)

Finding Love (Book 2)

Claire's Hope (Book 3)

Dylan's Faith (Book 4)

Stand Alones

Love Interrupted

Love Again

A Chance at Love

The Broken Road

If Only

Because Of You

The Lies We Believe

In His Love

When It Rains

Gracefully Broken

Please join T.K. Chapin's Mailing List to be notified
of upcoming releases and promotions.

<u>Join the List</u>

ACKNOWLEDGMENTS

First and foremost, I want to thank God. God's salvation through the death, burial and resurrection of Jesus Christ gives us all the ability to have a personal relationship with the Creator of the Universe.

I also want to thank my wife. She's my muse and my inspiration. A wonderful wife, an amazing mother and the best person I have ever met. She's great and has always stood by me with every decision I have made along life's way.

I'd like to thank my editors and early readers for helping me along the way. I also want to thank all of my friends and extended family for the support. It's a true blessing to have every person I know in my life.

ABOUT THE AUTHOR

 **T.K. CHAPIN** writes Christian Romance books designed to inspire and tug on your heart strings. He believes that telling stories of faith, love and family help build the faith of Christians and help non-believers see how God can work in the life of believers. He gives all credit for his writing and storytelling ability to God. The majority of the novels take place in and around Spokane, Washington, his hometown. Chapin makes his home in Idaho and has the pleasure of raising his daughter and two sons with his beautiful wife Crystal.

facebook.com/officialtkchapin

twitter.com/tkchapin

instagram.com/tkchapin

Made in the USA
Monee, IL
26 March 2020

23975446R00109